THE REBEL
PUBLISHING
HOUSE

Editing by
Swami Deva Ashik, M.A. (Oxon.)
Swami Krishna Prabhu
Typesetting by Ma Prem Arya
Design by Ma Dhyan Amiyo
Cover design by Swami Dhyan Suryam
Paintings by Ma Anand Meera
(Kasué Hashimoto), B.F.A.
(Musashino Art University, Tokyo)

Production by Swami Prem Visarjan
Printing by Mohndruck, Gütersloh
West Germany
Published by
The Rebel Publishing House GmbH
Cologne, West Germany
Copyright © Neo-Sannyas International
First Edition

ISBN 3-89338-065-5

In loving gratitude
to Osho Rajneesh
Rajneesh Foundation Australia

Talks given to the Rajneesh
International University of Mysticism
in Gautama the Buddha Auditorium
Poona, India
September 16–25, 1988

Dedicated to
Swami Sardar
Gurudayal Singh—
the only man
in the world
who laughs
before the joke
is told.
What a trust.

Osho Rajneesh
The Present Day
Awakened One
speaks on
the Ancient Masters
of Zen

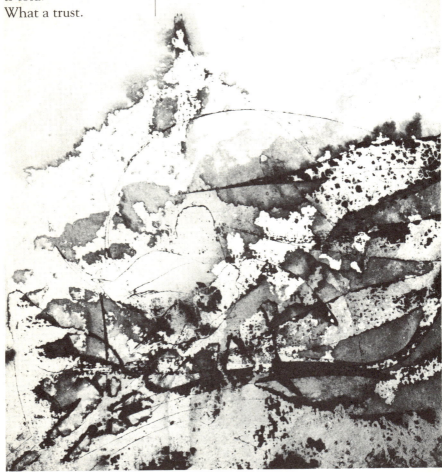

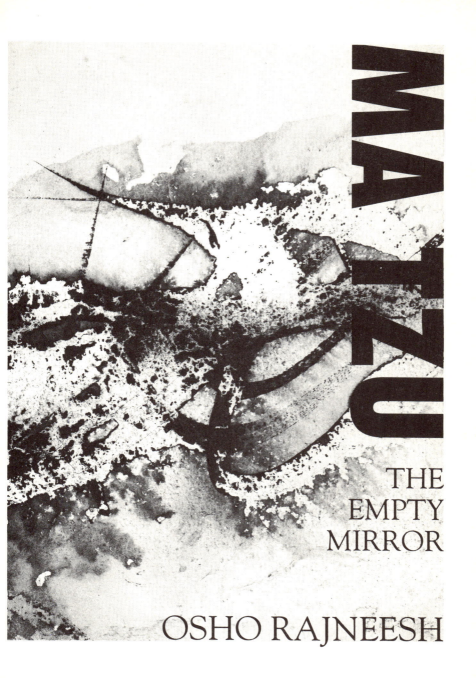

MA TZU

THE
EMPTY
MIRROR

OSHO RAJNEESH

I have called this series Ma Tzu: The Empty Mirror *for the simple reason that his whole teaching is, "Don't react. Just be, and reflect..."*

A simple summary of a simple teaching. Of course, in their

simplicity the words are vast and full of implications.

"Don't react." Is such a thing really possible? From the very beginning we are trained to react. "No"—and we learn to stop. "Hello" —and we learn to smile. And layers upon layers until we are just a jumble of conditioned reactions that we learn to call "myself."

Which brings us to, "Just be." Not a very popular idea. Just be *what*? A doctor, a lawyer, a good citizen? An American, a Japanese, a German? A good worker, a great genius, a famous artist? A Christian, a Buddhist?... No? Well, then *what*?

"And reflect"—like a mirror, not like the thinking process we

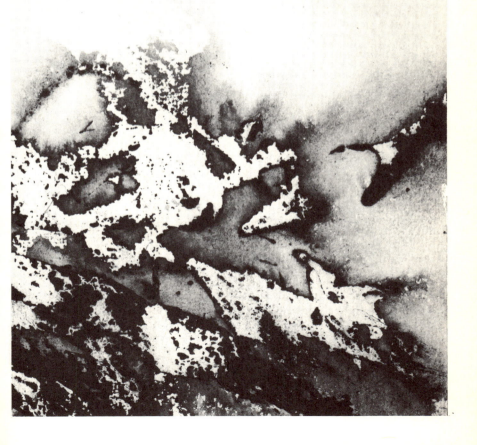

have come to associate with the word. Clearly, the first two are a prerequisite for the third; otherwise the American will continue to react like an American, the doctor will continue to view the world through a doctor's eyes, the Buddhist will follow his precepts and the Christian will follow Jesus. And we find ourselves back at the beginning of the circle—reacting to everything (yes, *everything*—even when somebody provokes us and we "don't react" we are actually most often suppressing a reaction that has already happened inside us) trying to be something, and "reflecting" like mad on what it all means.

And so it goes on. Some of us carry on doing it our whole lives, some of us go crazy, and some of us start searching for a way to jump off the wheel.

Osho Rajneesh is today, like Ma Tzu was in his day, a proof that jumping off the wheel is possible—and a reassurance that it will not, as we fear, bring multiple fractures and death, but rather a new wholeness and life.

Here in these pages you will not find the scholarly commentary which characterizes most books on Zen in the West—books which, in the effort to make Zen comprehensible to the rational mind, destroy its very message and add another layer to the very knowledgeability that Zen aims to strip away.

On the contrary, the 6th century Zen master Ma Tzu is not "explained" here—his work is continued and made fresh for the times in which we live. And in talking about Ma Tzu, Osho Rajneesh is talking about himself:

> *Existence creates a thirst only after it has created water to quench it. If there are disciples, seekers, searchers, existence manages that they should find a master who can see in them what is their possible future, and can help them to be themselves....*
>
> *One thinks at times that perhaps all these buddhas are just our imagination, because they have disappeared from our mundane world. Your function in being here is to bring that*

golden quest back into the world—and I am trying from all different angles, different approaches to the truth, hoping that something may click in you and open the door that has been closed for years, for centuries....

The door cracks open in these pages, a glimpse of the other side— off the wheel, where it is possible not to react but just to be, and reflect.

The living source of life is flowing just close by. Why not drink it and be quenched?

Ma Deva Sarito
Poona, 1989

The end of each discourse in this series follows a certain format which might be puzzling to the reader who has not been present at the event itself.

First is the time of Sardar Gurudayal Singh. "Sardarji" is a long-time disciple whose hearty and infectious laughter has resulted in the joke-telling time being named in his honor.

The jokes are followed by a meditation consisting of four parts. Each stage of the meditation is preceded by a signal from Osho to the drummer, Nivedano. This drumbeat is represented in the text as follows:

The first stage of the meditation is gibberish, which Osho has described as "cleansing your mind of all kinds of dust...speaking any language that you don't know...throwing all your craziness out." For several moments the hall goes completely mad, as thousands of people shout, scream, babble nonsense and wave their arms about.

The gibberish is represented in the text as follows:

The second stage is a period of silent sitting, of focusing the consciousness on the center, the point of witnessing.

The third stage is "let-go"—each person falls effortlessly to the ground, allowing the boundaries that keep them separate to dissolve.

A final drumbeat signals the assembly to return to a sitting position, as they are guided in making their experience of meditation more and more a part of everyday life. The participants are guided through each stage of the meditation by the words of the Master, and the entire text of each evening meditation is reproduced here.

Our Beloved Master,

When Nangaku first saw Ma Tzu, he recognized him by intuition as a vessel of the dharma.

He visited Ma Tzu in his cell where he was meditating, and asked him: "In practicing sitting meditation, what does your reverence aspire to attain?"

"To attain buddhahood" was Ma Tzu's reply.

Nangaku then took up a piece of brick and began to grind it against a rock

the mirror

in front of Ma Tzu's cell. Ma Tzu asked, "What are you grinding it for?"
"I want to grind it into a mirror," responded Nangaku.
Amused, Ma Tzu said, "How can you hope to grind a piece of brick into a mirror?"
Nangaku retorted, "Since a piece of brick cannot be ground into a mirror, how then can you sit yourself into a buddha?"
"What must I do then?" Ma Tzu asked.
Nangaku replied, "Take the case of an ox-cart: if the cart does not move, do you whip the cart or do you whip the ox?"
Ma Tzu remained silent.
"In learning sitting meditation," resumed Nangaku, "do you aspire to imitate the sitting Buddha or do you aspire to learn the sitting Zen? If the former, the Buddha has no fixed postures. If the latter, Zen does not consist in sitting or lying down.
"The dharma goes on forever and never abides in anything. You must not, therefore, be attached to, nor abandon, any particular phase of it. To sit yourself into Buddha is to kill the Buddha. To be attached to the sitting posture is to fail to comprehend the essential principle."

maneesha, we are starting a new series of talks: Ma Tzu—The Empty Mirror. Ma Tzu is also known as Baso. I am not using the name Baso, because our second series is going to be on the Japanese Bashō—the great mystic poet of Zen. And the name Ma Tzu is itself more meaningful than his popular name, Baso.

Before I discuss the sutras, a biographical note on Ma Tzu is absolutely needed, because he is not known to the world. He is one of those unfortunate geniuses whom the world tries in every way to ignore, to forget that they even exist. Even the idea that they exist hurts the ego of the crowd. It has been doing harm to every genius, because the very existence of a genius reduces you to a retarded being. Every enlightened master is evidence that you are living in darkness, that you have to transform your darkness into life, into light.

It seems to be such a great task—it is not, but it appears to be a great task—to transform your blindness into clear perceptive eyes; to transform your darkness into beautiful morning light. It is a simple thing, the simplest in the world, but just because it is simple, it does not appeal to the mind. Mind is interested in doing great things. The desire behind every ambition of the mind is to be special. And you can be special only with special achievements.

The problem with Zen is that it wants you to be utterly simple, not special. It goes against the very desire of the mind, which is not a small phenomenon—it is a four-million-years-old desire, which everybody is carrying in different lives. Mind cannot understand why you should be simple when you could be special, why you should be humble when you could be powerful. And mind is heavy, it has the great weight of the past. The moment the mind sees anyone humble, simple, natural, a buddha, it immediately condemns him, because such a man goes against the whole makeup of the human mind.

And in a way the mind is right. To be a buddha you will have to drop the mind completely, you will have to become an empty mirror.

Ma Tzu was born in China in the year 709. He was the most important figure in the history of Zen after the sixth patriarch, Enō. Enō told Nangaku, who would become Ma Tzu's master, about a prophecy that Nangaku would have "a spirited young horse" of a disciple who would "trample the whole world." In Chinese, the 'Ma' of Ma Tzu means 'horse'.

As a child, Ma Tzu joined a local monastery; before he was twenty, he was already a professed monk.

He was a born genius, and even had prophecies about him by other masters—that he is not to be taken as just XYZ, he has a possibility of becoming a great master—and the prophecies were fulfilled.

Sometimes it is possible, if a master looks at a child when the child is still uncorrupted by the society, that he can see his potential clearly. And that's what another great master, Enō, said to Nangaku.

Enō was the sixth patriarch, the sixth great master after Bodhidharma. He told Nangaku, "This child is going to become a great master; be careful." And finally Ma Tzu became not only a great master, but the second most important master after Enō. Enō's prophecy was fulfilled more than he had expected. Ma Tzu proved himself to be a greater master than the prophecy had said.

But it is his strange fate that he is not known to the world. Perhaps he was too much ahead of his time; perhaps he was too far away from the ordinary crowd; perhaps his way of teaching was so subtle that the ordinary mind was incapable of comprehending it.

But whatever the cause, we are resurrecting Ma Tzu. We want him to be accepted in the history of consciousness, in the place that belongs to him.

The story Maneesha has brought:
When Nangaku first saw Ma Tzu, he recognized him by intuition as a vessel of the dharma.
A master is nothing but clarity, transparency. To him, things which are invisible to you are visible. Your potentiality is something very invisible, the mystery of your being. But to the master it is almost an open book; he can read it. And to have such a master, who can read your potentiality and can help you grow according to your potentiality—not according to his ideology—is the greatest blessing one can have.
When Nangaku first saw Ma Tzu, he recognized him by intuition as a vessel of the dharma.
These are metaphors. "A vessel of the dharma" is to say that he will become a presence which will send a radiation all around. People will come from thousands of miles away, pulled by an invisible force, like gravitation, not knowing why they are being pulled to a certain person. They will understand only when they have reached to that person—felt his energy, quenched their thirst. Then they will know that some subtle force was pulling them to fulfill their destiny.

Just a few days ago, I came to know that trees have a certain sensibility about water. The scientist who was exploring it was amazed to see that there was a tree with no water around, except that two hundred feet away there was a water pipe. But the tree sent its roots to the water pipe, forced it to break, and was relishing and nourishing itself from that water.

The scientist was worried because he could not find any water around the tree, and he had not thought that it was carrying the water from a water pipe that it had broken with its roots. He was

6

puzzled—how did the tree know about the water pipe two hundred feet away? And it had not sent its roots anywhere else, just directly to the water pipe.

The tree cannot live without water. Certainly it must have a certain sensibility, a certain hidden knowledge where water is, even though the water is inside a pipe, and two hundred feet away.

The same is the situation with you, if your quest for truth is honest, not just a curiosity. From thousands of miles away, you will start getting pulled to a place where your thirst can be quenched. Existence makes a thirst only after it has created water to quench it. If there are disciples, seekers, searchers, existence manages that they should find a master who can see in them what their possible future is, and can help them to be themselves.

The master has no ideology, the master is not a missionary, the master does not program you. On the contrary he *de*-programs you; he takes away all your ideologies, your prejudices, your very mind, so that the pure emptiness of your being starts growing.

The masters have been lost, the whole world of that golden quest for truth has become a memory. And at times one thinks, "Perhaps all these buddhas are just our imagination"—because they have disappeared from our mundane world.

Your purpose in being here is to bring that golden quest back into the world. And I am trying from all different angles—all these masters are different angles, different approaches to the truth—hoping that something may click in you and open the door that has been closed for years, for centuries.

He visited Ma Tzu in his cell where he was meditating, and asked him: "In practicing sitting meditation, what does your reverence aspire to attain?"

Just take note of it: Nangaku was a well-established master and Ma Tzu was just a young disciple, but he addresses him as "your reverence." For the master, your present is not only the present, it is also your future. He knows you, that one day you will become a buddha. It does not matter that it takes a few days, or a few years, or a few lives. Because Nangaku can see his buddhahood, he addresses even a disciple as "your reverence."

It reminds me about Gautam Buddha's past life, when he was not yet a buddha, and he heard about a great master who had become enlightened. He went to see, just out of curiosity, what this phenomenon of enlightenment is, and how it makes a difference in a man.

He touched the feet of the man, although he had no intention of doing so; but just as he came into his energy field, spontaneously he touched his feet. He wondered why he was touching his feet, because he had not come there to be a disciple. But the very area, the very atmosphere, the very milieu—and something in his heart started ringing a bell, that perhaps he had come close to his home, without any conscious intention.

Just spontaneously he touched the feet of the man. It was a miracle to him, because he had never touched anybody's feet. He was not a man of faith or belief; he was a young man, and very argumentative. This was a strange act that he had done, but stranger than this was that when he stood up, the master touched *his* feet.

He said, "What are you doing? In the first place, I had no idea, no desire, no intention of touching your feet—but it happened. I was just watching it happening in spite of me. And now you are touching my feet!—I am nobody, I don't know even the ABC of enlightenment. I have just come here out of curiosity."

The master said, "You may not know what is contained in your seed, but I know. I can see that one day you are going to become the buddha. Yesterday I was not a buddha, today I am a buddha; today you are not a buddha, tomorrow you will be a buddha. This small time difference does not make any difference."

Nangaku said to Ma Tzu, who was meditating in his cell, *"In practicing sitting meditation, what does your reverence aspire to attain?"*

"To attain buddhahood" was Ma Tzu's reply.

It has to be understood that buddhahood cannot be attained, it is already your nature. If you try to attain it, you will miss it. You have just to relax and see within yourself, and the buddha is already there in its absolute splendor.

The use of the word 'attain' means that something has to be done, you have to go somewhere. There is a possibility of failure—you may succeed, you may not succeed. And attainment is always of the outside world, of the objective world—riches, or fame, or power....

But buddhahood is not an attainment. It is simply a remembrance, as if you had forgotten something, and suddenly in a silent relaxed state you remember it.

I think every one of you must have come at one time or other to the experience when you know that you know something, and you say that it is just on the tip of your tongue, but still you cannot remember. A very strange and weird feeling arises at that time. You know somebody's name—you are absolutely sure that you know, you can even close your eyes and see the person—you feel that the name is just on your tongue, but you are stuck there, it is not becoming expressed.

It is a very weird feeling—that you know it, and you know that you know, and yet you cannot express it. It is just on the tip of your tongue, but the more you try, the more it becomes difficult.

The reason is that every effort makes your mind tense; and the more the mind is tense, the more it becomes closed. What is needed ...you should go into the garden, and start digging or watering the plants, and forget all about this fellow who you remember and who is just sitting on the tip of your tongue. Just simply spit it out. Get engaged in something simple—watering the roses; and while you are watering the roses, the mind will start relaxing. The closedness will start opening, and suddenly, from nowhere, the name has bubbled up to the surface.

While you were trying it was not possible for you to get it. But when you were not trying, and you simply dropped the idea of getting it, it came back with such a rushing force.

To be a buddha is exactly like that.

All that I teach you is not a philosophy, it cannot even be called a teaching. I simply help you to relax to such a point where you can remember what you have forgotten completely.

That remembrance will make you aware of your buddhahood.

That remembrance is not an achievement because the buddha is already within you; hence the word 'attainment' is not right. But Ma

Tzu's reply can be understood with a little more compassion. He does not know what exactly buddhahood is, he just has a feeling that there is something to be found, there is something missing in his life, to give it meaning and significance.

The word 'buddha' simply signifies that he is searching for awareness. But because he does not know that what he is searching for is within himself, it is absolutely possible for him to use the word 'attainment'. He is using the wrong word, but his longing is right. He is on the right path, he is just using a wrong word. And you have to forgive him because he is only a seeker, he is not a master yet.

Nangaku then took up a piece of brick and began to grind it against a rock in front of Ma Tzu's cell. Ma Tzu asked, "What are you grinding it for?"

This will give you some feel of how Zen masters have been unique in their efforts to awaken their disciples. This is a strange way, but spontaneous, because nobody else has done it before, nor afterwards. Only Nangaku did it.

Ma Tzu asked, "What are you grinding it for?"

"I want to grind it into a mirror," responded Nangaku.

Amused, Ma Tzu said, "How can you hope to grind a piece of brick into a mirror?"

Nangaku retorted, "Since a piece of brick cannot be ground into a mirror, how then can you sit yourself into a buddha?"

"How can you—remaining yourself, sitting here in the cell—become the buddha? Neither the brick can become a mirror, nor just by sitting can you become a buddha. You can have the same posture as the buddha, the same lotus posture, but just sitting like him does not mean that you become him. Your effort is as futile as my effort of making a brick into a mirror."

What he is saying in fact is that you cannot become the mirror just by grinding your mind. What are you doing here? Just grinding your mind, and trying to make a mirror of it. The buddha is the mirror; the buddha simply reflects, he does not react. He is always empty like a mirror. Things come and go before the mirror, but they don't leave any trace on the mirror.

"What must I do then?" Ma Tzu asked.

Nangaku replied, "Take the case of an ox-cart: if the cart does not move, do you whip the cart or do you whip the ox?"
Ma Tzu remained silent.
"In learning sitting meditation," resumed Nangaku, "do you aspire to imitate the sitting Buddha or do you aspire to learn the sitting Zen? If the former, the Buddha has no fixed postures"—sometimes he stands up, sometimes he walks, and sometimes he sleeps also—*"If the latter, Zen does not consist in sitting or lying down. The dharma goes on forever and never abides in anything."*

It has no particular form, it has no particular place; it goes on moving into different forms. You will not be able to find it in any form, in any body, in any posture. You will have to look within. It is only found in the emptiness, because emptiness cannot sit, cannot stand up, cannot lie down. Emptiness is just emptiness; it is eternally empty. That is the only thing that is eternal—your empty heart.

"The dharma goes on forever and never abides in anything.
You must not, therefore, be attached to, nor abandon,
any particular phase of it.
To sit yourself into Buddha is to kill the Buddha."

It is the majesty of Zen to say things directly, straightforwardly. No other religion has that courage.

Nangaku is saying to Ma Tzu, *"To sit yourself into Buddha"*—taking the buddha posture—*"is to kill the Buddha."* Don't murder…

Before dying Gautam Buddha said to his disciples, "Don't make statues of me, because that will give a wrong impression to people. They will think that if you sit in this posture, you will become a buddha."

But who hears? Today there are more statues of Buddha than of anybody else. In fact, in languages like Arabic, Persian, Urdu—because Mohammedans are against statues—the word for statue is 'budt'; and 'budt' is just a form of 'buddha'. In Sanskrit 'buddh' is the original root of buddha—to be aware. From 'buddh' it is very easy to make 'budt'.

This happened because Mohammedans came across more statues of Buddha than of anybody else. And they were destroying statues; wherever they went they were destroying statues. They destroyed

11

beautiful pieces of art. To be against statues does not mean that you have to destroy statues.

You can see in this way how the unconscious mind moves from one extreme to another extreme. Gautam Buddha said, "Don't make statues of me, because people may think that just by sitting in the lotus posture you can become aware. Just leave it like this—that awareness has no form, you have to find it within you. You cannot find it in a buddha statue. Do not distract them by outside statues —because man's mind is such that it can be distracted by anything, it becomes attached to anything…."

I have heard about a Buddhist nun who had her own small statue of Gautam Buddha, made of solid gold, and she used to carry it while she was traveling from monastery to monastery. But her problem was that every morning she would worship her buddha, and she would burn incense—but incense cannot be directed, it may go to some other buddha in the temple. Now this was very bad—her own buddha was sitting there, and the incense and the perfume that she offered had flown away to some other buddha.

There used to be—there still are—temples with many buddhas. And she was so much attached to her own buddha that it became a problem. Her buddha and other buddhas…

She finally found a strategy so that the incense reached to her buddha—because she was offering her incense, and the other buddhas were getting it. She made a small bamboo, just like a hollow passage, and she kept it on her incense burner, moving the perfume with the hollow bamboo towards the nose of her own buddha.

But then there arose another problem: the nose of her buddha became black. She was in great distress; a gold buddha, a solid gold buddha, with a black nose—it does not suit. He looks almost like a nigger…!

She inquired of the older monks, "What to do now? If I don't put the bamboo there, the incense…nobody knows where it goes. It goes to all kinds of buddhas; but I am offering it to *my* buddha. And now because of this bamboo, the nose and a part of the face have become black. What should I do?"

The monk she was asking laughed and said, "You are an idiot

woman! You don't understand the simple fact that all the buddhas are the same, they are statues of the same person. You have become attached to your buddha, and the whole teaching of Buddha is non-attachment.

"It is perfectly right; Buddha has shown you that attachment makes you dirty. So beware of it! Just go to a goldsmith so he can clean and polish your buddha. But from now onwards, just think of *the* Buddha. Any buddha, whichever buddha gets the incense...perhaps he deserves it! And you should be happy that it has reached to somebody, because all those statues represent the same person."

Buddhists, the followers of Buddha, did not hear his last words, "Don't make statues of me. Let me represent the formless; only the fragrance, not the flower."

And there has been another extreme. Mohammed was against statues, because if you worship a statue...it is a stone, and worshipping a stone is a barrier to the worship of God. So all barriers have to be removed.

It was perfectly okay if somebody was willing to remove it, but Mohammedans started removing other people's barriers. They forgot all about God. Their whole history became a destruction of statues.

Neither by worshipping a statue can you reach to the buddha, nor by destroying statues can you reach to the buddha. You have to go withinwards; outside there is nothing that can give you the eternal, the ultimate, the truth that can quench your thirst.

"To sit yourself into Buddha is to kill the Buddha. To be attached to the sitting posture is to fail to comprehend the essential principle."

The essential principle is never objective; it is your subjectivity. The essential principle has no form; it is absolute emptiness. The essential principle is a mirror; it only reflects, it does not make any judgment of good or bad, of beauty or ugliness.

Chi-Hsien wrote:

I possess potentiality;
it is seen in a blink.
He who does not understand
cannot be called a monk.

It applies to you exactly the way it was applicable to Chi-Hsien's disciples. *I possess potentiality; it is seen in a blink.* It is not a far away phenomenon. Just close your eyes, and look silently, deep, and it is there. It has been there for eternity, just waiting for you to come home.

Maneesha has asked:

Our Beloved Master,
Are we all, the ten thousand buddhas, potential vessels of the dharma?

Maneesha, as far as being potential vessels of dharma, nobody is an exception. You all have the potential—the same potential, the same highest peaks of consciousness, as any buddha. But you have to go inwards and find your treasures. Outside you are a beggar, everybody is a beggar.

Alexander the Great came to India just three hundred years after Buddha had died. He wanted to meet some master. The name and the fame of Buddha had reached faraway shores—even to Greece and Athens.

Alexander's master was the father of Western logic, Aristotle. Aristotle had told him, "You are going to conquer the world, you must reach India. I don't want you to bring anything as a present for me, just meet an enlightened master. I have heard so much, but it seems to be so ungraspable. And moreover, because I am a logician, I cannot accept anything unless it is rationally valid, with evidence, argument."

On his way back, Alexander remembered that he had to find a master. He inquired of people and they said, "It is very difficult. Even if you can find a master, we don't think he will be agreeable to going with you to Greece."

Alexander said, "Don't be worried about that. If I want to take the Himalayas to Greece, I can manage it!"

Finally he found a master. Many people had said, "Yes, that person is a realized one. He lives naked by the side of the river."

Alexander reached to the man, and with his naked sword he said, "I want you to come with me! You will be given a royal welcome; every facility will be available to you. You will be a royal guest, so don't be worried about anything. But I want you to come to Greece, because my master wants to see an enlightened man."

The old man laughed. He said, "In the first place, put your sword back into its sheath—this is not the way to meet a master. And get down from your horse!"

Alexander had never heard such authoritative words—and from a naked man, who has nothing.

And the man said, "Remember that you may conquer the whole world, but you are still a beggar. Now you are begging me to come with you. But as far as I'm concerned, I have come to the point where there is no movement. I don't go anywhere, I have never gone anywhere. I have been always now and here. Time has stopped, mind has stopped...."

Alexander was very angry. He said, "I will cut off your head if you don't come with me!"

The man said, "That's a good idea. You can take the head, but I'm not coming. And remember: just as you cut off my head, you will be watching the head falling on the ground and I will also be watching. Watching is our secret, tell your master—and take my head."

Now it is very difficult to take the head of such a man, who is not afraid at all. Alexander said, "I have to go without a master."

The old man said, "Tell your master that enlightenment is not something that you can bring from outside. You cannot export it—you have to explore it within yourself. Drop all logic, all rationality, all mind, and go inwards as deep as you can. At the very end of your search you will find the buddha.

"My coming will be of no use. I would not have refused, because there is no difference for me, where I am—but seeing me, do you see any enlightenment? Neither will your master be able to see any enlightenment. To see enlightenment, you need a little bit of the experience of enlightenment, at least some meditativeness. And I don't think meditation has even entered into the consciousness of people in the West."

Strangely, even today—the twenty-three hundred years since Alexander have not been of any help—meditation is still an Eastern concept. It is still only in the East that people become thirsty to inquire within.

My effort is to spread the fire all over the world, to destroy the distinction between East and West. But every hindrance is being created. You all have to take the fire of meditation to your countries. Just small beginnings, and soon it can become a wildfire.

Except for meditation there is no way to know yourself—in your purity, in your utter innocence, just like a mirror. But you are all vessels of the dharma, of the basic principle. You may recognize it, you may not recognize it. You are carrying it, you are pregnant with it —whether you give birth or not, that is a different matter. Just a little relaxation, just a little looking inwards, and the doors of immense potentialities open up. You are no more a beggar. Without conquering the world you have conquered the whole universe.

Just conquer yourself.

The rains have come to hear your laughter. (*A loud and familiar laugh is heard from the back of the auditorium.*) And Sardar Gurudayal Singh has started it.

Three sannyasin kids meet in the ashram and start talking together.

"You know," says the German kid, "my uncle is a priest, and all the people call him 'holy father.'"

"That's nothing," says the Japanese kid. "My grandfather is a Zen master, and even the emperor touches his feet."

"That's nothing, you guys," says the American kid. "My mother weighs three hundred pounds, and when she walks down the street, people take one look at her and say, '*My God!*'"

Father Finger has a little trouble with a sixteen-year-old blonde and the police. He goes immediately to see his lawyer, Boris Babblebrain. "If you win the case for me," says Finger, "I'll give you a thousand dollars."

"Okay," agrees Babblebrain, "get some witnesses."

Father Finger searches around his parish and manages to find two old drunks and a bag lady for his witnesses. They tell the right story, and he wins the case.

"I won your case for you," says Babblebrain. "Now, what about my thousand dollars?"

"Okay," replies Father Finger, "just get some witnesses!"

At a chic cocktail party in Hollywood, Sheikh Ali Baba, the fabulously rich oil millionaire, meets Brenda Babblebrain and falls madly in love with her.

Sheikh Ali Baba approaches her husband, Boris, the lawyer, and leads him into a quiet corner.

"I must sleep with your wife," says Ali Baba, "and in return, I will pay you her weight in gold."

Boris hesitates, and then he insists that he will need a few days.

"To think the deal over?" asks Ali Baba, anxiously.

"No, no!" cries Boris, "to fatten her up!"

Nivedano...

Nivedano...

Be silent.
Let your body be completely frozen.
Close your eyes, and look inwards
with as much urgency and totality as possible.
Deeper and deeper...
you are entering the space we call the buddha.
This beautiful evening can become
a great radical change in your life,
if you are courageous enough to go on,
just like an arrow,
to the very center of your being.
You are just a witness,
an empty mirror.

To make it more clear, Nivedano...

Relax.
Watch—the body is not you, the mind is not you.
Only the watching, only the witnessing is you.
This witnessing is your eternity.
With this witnessing comes all the ecstasies,

all the blessings that existence can offer to you.
The deeper you are, the more watchful you are—
the more silent, the more peaceful.
It is a great event.
Every evening you go a little deeper into your
buddhahood.
Look around this empty space within you;
you have to remember it, twenty-four hours,
when you come back from the inner journey.

Nivedano...

Come back, but come back as buddhas—
peaceful, silent, graceful, with a beatitude.
Sit down for a few moments just as mirrors;
remembering your inner world,
collecting the experience so that
it can become an undercurrent in your daily life.
I don't want anybody to escape from life;
I want everybody to make life richer,
more blissful, more ecstatic.
I am all for life,
because to me life is the only God.
The buddha is another name for life.

Okay, Maneesha?
Yes, Beloved Master.
Can we celebrate the ten thousand buddhas?
Yes, Beloved Master.

sowing
seed

Our Beloved Master,

After his first instructions from his master, Nangaku, on the meaning of the dharma, Ma Tzu felt as if he were drinking the most exquisite nectar. After bowing to the master, Ma Tzu asked him, "How must one be attuned to the formless samadhi?"

The master said, "When you cultivate the way of interior wisdom, it is like sowing seed. When I expound to you the essentials of dharma, it is like the

showers from heaven. As you are receptive to the teaching, you are destined to see the Tao."
Ma Tzu again asked: "Since the Tao is beyond color and form, how can it be seen?"
The master said: "The dharma-eye of your interior spirit is capable of perceiving the Tao. So it is with the formless samadhi."
"Is there still making and unmaking?" Ma Tzu asked.
To this, the master replied, "If one sees the Tao from the standpoint of making and unmaking, or gathering and scattering, one does not really see the Tao. Listen to my gatha:

"The ground of the no-mind
contains many seeds
which will all sprout when
heavenly showers come.
The flower of samadhi
is beyond color and form.
How can there be any more
mutability?"

It is said that at this, Ma Tzu was truly enlightened, his mind having transcended the world of phenomena. He attended upon his master for a full ten years. During this period, he delved deeper and deeper into meditation.

maneesha, a great master on his own authority, Nangaku, is working on a greater master, Ma Tzu, who is just a seed right now, but contains a great buddha.

You are also seeds. It is up to you if you remain closed. Then you will never know your ultimate nature as a buddha. A little courage, a little opening, a little dying of the cover of the seed and the buddha starts sprouting in you.

You cannot blame the climate. The rains are there. The clouds have even entered into the auditorium, they are just passing before my eyes. So close are the clouds...but the strange thing is that the closer the clouds are, the more the seed becomes afraid. Afraid of the unknown, afraid of...one never knows what is going to be outside. Hidden inside a cover, the seed feels safer, more secure.

On the path of Zen you have to learn these important words: openness, joy in insecurity—a challenge from the unknown has always to be welcomed. That is the way of growing up. Most of the people in the world, who Wilhelm Reich has called "little men," die as little men, although their destiny is not to be little men. Wilhelm Reich was perfectly right in respect of the masses, the crowd, to call his book *Listen, Little Man*. But he was absolutely wrong because he could not see that hidden in the little man is the greatest buddha.

He simply condemned the little man because all the little men were condemning him. He was a genius; not a buddha but an intellectual giant, and he has been condemned by the crowds. Finally he was forced within the walls of a madhouse. And he was saying immensely sensible things. He was bringing a new territory to be explored.

But all those fearful people, afraid of the unknown, afraid of losing the security and the safety of the bank balance, forced him into a madhouse. And he was not mad. In his madhouse days he wrote his best books. They are evidence that he was not mad. But the politicians and the crowd and the government all conspired to force him to live in a madhouse. They all laughed at his immensely valuable discoveries about human energy. Naturally he was angry.

So when he wrote the book *Listen, Little Man*, it was not out of compassion, it was out of reaction. They had done harm to him, and he at least was able to condemn them. His book is beautiful in describing the little man. But the essential part of the little man is the seed, his potentiality, which Reich completely forgets in his anger.

Otherwise he was very close to becoming enlightened. But in his anger, his reaction, he was incapable of seeing the point that the people were bound to condemn him—his being a genius was enough reason for their condemnation. They were bound to crucify him and it had to be understood as the natural course of things. But he could not take it as the natural course of things. He could not understand that it is something that has to happen to every genius who opens the doors of insecurity.

And because of this great cloud of anger, he was completely blind, unable to see that the little man is a buddha, hidden deep down as a seed.

Nangaku is instructing Ma Tzu.
After his first instructions from his master, Nangaku, on the meaning of the dharma, Ma Tzu felt as if he were drinking the most exquisite nectar. After bowing to the master, Ma Tzu asked him, "How must one be attuned to the formless samadhi?"
The first thing to understand is the meaning of *dharma*. Unfortunately the Sanskrit word 'dharma'—or the Pali word which Buddha used, 'dhamma'—has been wrongly translated as 'religion' by the theologians, and by scholars it has been translated as 'law', the ultimate law. Both have missed the point.

Dharma is not religion. In fact if you go to the roots of the words, religion means that which binds you, and dharma means that which frees you. They are absolutely contrary to each other. Dharma simply means your intrinsic nature. It is not written in scriptures and nobody can tell you what your dharma is. You have to find it yourself. This is a great dignity, conferred on the individual by existence, that you don't have to live on borrowed knowledge. The living source of life is just flowing close by. Why not drink it and be quenched?

Ma Tzu says, after understanding the meaning of the dharma, that *he felt as if he were drinking the most exquisite nectar.* The deeper you go in your meditations, the closer you will come to the eternal stream of your life sources. It is pure nectar, because it declares your immortality, it declares your eternity. It declares that death is a fiction; it has never happened and will never happen to anyone. One only changes the house; one gets into another form or maybe into the formless existence.

Ma Tzu's statement that *he felt as if he were drinking the most exquisite nectar* shows his tremendous understanding. He is very new in meditation, he is so young. But age has nothing to do with your realization. It is not that when you get old, you will be able to become a buddha easily. On the contrary, the older you become the more difficult it becomes for you to drop your lifelong habits, concepts, ideologies.

Just two years ago Pope the Polack was in India and he was surprised to see that the very poor and the orphans who have been converted to Christianity were doing the same in their churches as they had been doing before: burning incense, bringing flowers for Jesus Christ. He could not believe what the priests were doing, because these people were doing exactly what they used to do in their temples. Instead of Krishna, now Christ is there, everything else is the same.

But the priests told him that they had to make a few considerations, a few compromises. These people cannot understand a religion without incense, without flowers. And the pope conceded that for Indian Christians it is okay.

As you become old, it becomes very difficult to change your ideology, your lifelong belief. It becomes hardened. The old man becomes hard, and in the same way everything around him becomes hard. The best situation in which to grow into your potential is childhood. Next to it is your youth. Most probably the childhood will be spoilt by the parents, by the priests.

The authentic religion has to depend on youth, because youth has a certain rebelliousness natural to it. A young man can rebel against the whole past without any guilt. He can clean his heart of all the old dead scriptures and statues, and the challenge of the unknown stirs his heart. He wants to accept the greatest challenge, and this is the greatest challenge in life—to allow your seed to open to the unknown skies, to the winds, the sun, the rain; one never knows what is going to happen.

There is nobody to guide the seed, there are no scriptures for the seed to read. The seed is taking a risk by coming out, and you should understand that the risk is not small. The risk is exactly a death. The seed has to die in the soil; only then the sprouts of the potentiality of the seed will start growing. Perhaps it will become a roseflower, or a lotus, or some other kind of flower. It does not matter. What matters is flowering, not the name of the flower. A wild flower is as beautiful as the most precious rose. They are brothers in one way, that they both have come to their flowering. They have both enjoyed the joy of growth, they both have seen with their own eyes what was hidden in their seed. They have both taken the same risk and the same challenge.

In fact it is a death and a resurrection. The seed dies and resurrects into many flowers, into many fruits, into many seeds. It is said that a single seed can make the whole earth green. Just one plant is not its potential. On that one plant there will come thousands of seeds again, each seed again carrying thousands of seeds.

Just a single seed can fill the whole earth with absolute greenness. Such tremendous possibility in a small seed! And you are a living seed, conscious. The most precious thing in existence is within you: consciousness. The seed is groping in the dark, still finding the way. And you are conscious, you have a little light, but you don't move from your position, you remain a little man. In fact you hate all those who have gone to the other shore because their very going condemns you, that you have failed to fulfill your own destiny.

After bowing to the master, Ma Tzu asked him, "How must one be attuned to the formless samadhi?"

The master must have said to him that unless you become attuned with existence in utter silence, you cannot know the dharma, the very principle of life and existence. Ma Tzu's inquiry is that of an honest seeker. He loved what was said, he felt it as if it was exquisite nectar—but he would not believe it. There are still things to be settled. His question is not the question of a student, it is the question of a would-be master.

"How must one be attuned to formless samadhi?"

He cuts out all unnecessary questions and comes exactly to the right thing, how one should be attuned to the formless *samadhi*.

Samadhi is a Sanskrit word, very beautiful in its meaning. It comes from a root which means, when there is no question and no answer, when your silence is so profound that you don't even have the question; answers are left far away but you don't have even the question. Such innocence which is just silent is called samadhi. And in this samadhi you can fall in tune with the heartbeat of the universe. Only in samadhi can you become one with the whole. There is no other way.

Every day what we are doing in the name of meditation is moving towards samadhi. Meditation is the beginning and samadhi is the end. Ma Tzu's question is that of a potential buddha. He is not asking about non-essentials, just the very essential.

The master said, "When you cultivate the way of interior wisdom, it is like sowing seed. When I expound to you the essentials of dharma, it is like the showers from heaven. As you are receptive to the teaching, you are destined to see the Tao."

Tao is Chinese for what we call samadhi; the Japanese call it *satori*, the Chinese call it *Tao*. Tao is perhaps the best of all these expressions, because it is not part of language. It simply indicates something inexpressible, something that you can know but cannot say, something that you can live but cannot explain. It is something that you can dance, you can sing, but you cannot utter a single word about it. You can be it; you can be the expression of Tao, but you cannot say what it is that you are expressing.

Ma Tzu again asked: "Since the Tao is beyond color and form, how can it be seen?"

You have to understand this dialogue very deeply, because it will give you the right direction for what has to be asked. There are thousands of things to ask, but the essentials are very few and unless you start by asking the essentials, you will not come close to the truth.

As Nangaku mentioned the Tao, Ma Tzu immediately asked: *"Since the Tao is beyond color and form, how can it be seen?—*you are saying that if you enter into samadhi, you will see the Tao."

The master said: "The dharma-eye of your interior spirit is capable of perceiving the Tao. So it is with the formless samadhi."

It was for this reason that the East had to develop the concept of the third eye. These two eyes can see only the form, the color, but they cannot see the formless and the colorless. For the formless and colorless they are blind. In samadhi you close these eyes and a new perceptivity, which can be metaphorically called 'the third eye', arises in you; a new sensitivity which can feel and see what is not possible for your outer senses.

The dharma-eye, which is the third eye of your interior spirit, is capable of perceiving the Tao. When I say to you in meditations, "Go deeper, look deeper," I am trying in every way so that your third eye, which has remained dormant, opens up.

Ma Tzu still asked, *"Is there still making and unmaking?"*

Can we do something inside? Can we make a buddha inside? Is there still some creativity inside? It is a very profound question.

To this, the master replied, "If one sees the Tao from the standpoint of making and unmaking, or gathering and scattering, one does not really see the Tao. Listen to my gatha."

He says that as far as your inner world is concerned your buddha is already there; you don't have to make it. Everything is as it should be in your inner world.

I am reminded of the Russian scientist, Kirlian, who brought a new vision to the objective scientist; its implications are immense. He was a great photographer and he went on perfecting and refining his lenses. His whole idea was that if something is hidden in a seed as a potential, then perhaps the photograph of the potential can be caught with a better lens.

It was a very strange idea, but scientists and mystics and philosophers and poets are all a little bit crazy. Everybody tried to persuade him: "Don't do such nonsense, how can you see the rose in the seed?"

He said, "If it is going to be, then it must be present in some way —perhaps our eyes are not capable of seeing it." And finally he succeeded. He managed to create lenses which could take a photograph of what was going to happen in the future. He would put the seed in front of his camera and a photograph would come of a rose flower.

And then he would wait for the seed to die into the soil—and it was one of the miracles of modern genius, that when the real rose came, it would be exactly the same as the photograph. He has caught the future in his net.

He became convinced that if it is true about the seed then it can be used in many things. For example, Kirlian photography has now become an absolute must in Russian hospitals. People come just to be checked, to see if there is any possibility of disease in the future.

His lenses have become even more refined now after his death; a whole school of Kirlian photographers has been working on it. They can see at least six months ahead. If you are going to be sick in six months' time, the photograph will show it—that after six months you will have cancer. There is no other way to find it out, but it can be treated although it has not become manifest. It is a tremendous blessing to medicine. We can cure people before they become sick.

What we see with our eyes is not all. Even in the outside world our eyes have limitations. Kirlian photography has gone beyond our eyes into the objective world. In the same way the third eye opens in the inner world and brings you your whole potentiality in its fullness. You don't have to do anything, you have just to recognize it. A buddha is not made, a buddha is only remembered.

Nangaku said, *"Listen to my gatha."* That is an ancient way; 'gatha' means poetry. "What I could manage to say in prose, I have said. Now listen to my poetry. Something that I have not been able to say in prose can be said in poetry.

"The ground of the no-mind
contains many seeds
which will all sprout when
heavenly showers come."

They have come and now it is up to you to take the challenge.

"The flower of samadhi
is beyond color and form.
How can there be any more
mutability?"

It is said that at this, Ma Tzu was truly enlightened, his mind having transcended the world of phenomena. He attended upon his master for a full ten years. During this period, he delved deeper and deeper into meditation.

Kanzan wrote:

In my house there is a cave,
and in the cave is nothing at all—
pure and wonderfully empty,
resplendent, with a light
like the sun.
A meal of greens will do
for this old body,
a ragged coat will cover

this phantom form.
Let a thousand saints appear
before me—I have the
buddha of heavenly truth!

Once you have looked into your inner cave and found the light, the life, the very source of your being, then the so-called saints don't mean anything. They are just moralists, following a certain system of morality, beliefs, but they don't have the truth. If you have the truth then even a thousand saints cannot weigh more than your buddha. Your buddha is the ultimate and it is not borrowed. You have discovered it.

Maneesha has asked:

Our Beloved Master,
I love the expression, "Take one step towards Allah, and he will come running a thousand steps towards you."
It seems to suggest that receptivity is not a totally inactive waiting but requires a certain participation.
Even to receive a flower, doesn't one need to hold out one's hand? Or am I on the wrong track again?

Yes, Maneesha, you are on a wrong track again. That saying comes from Mohammedanism, "Take one step towards Allah, and he will come running a thousand steps toward you."

But in the world of Zen there is no Allah, and as far as your inside is concerned, just take one step and you *are* the Allah. Nobody comes running. On the contrary, you come to a standstill. Just one step, inside—that Mohammedan saying is still about the outside God—you take one step and God will come running towards you. But that kind of God does not exist, so don't unnecessarily waste your step! Save it, you will need it to go in. And the moment you go one step in, you are the Allah. In the world of Zen that kind of statement is not applicable at all.

Now the clouds have come, really with tremendous urgency! This year Poona is going to be flooded even without the Shankaracharya committing suicide. Just the laughter of ten thousand buddhas is enough to call all the clouds of the world. They don't need any passport, any visa. They don't have to pass any customs office. They are the free buddhas moving in the sky, and when they see ten thousand buddhas gathered, naturally they come running—particularly at the time when I am going to tell you the jokes.

Where is Sardar Gurudayal Singh? Just laugh loudly. This book is going to be dedicated to Sardar Gurudayal Singh, the only man in history who laughs before the joke is told. What a trust! You should learn trust from Sardar Gurudayal Singh.

Maggie MacTavish dies and leaves old Hamish a widower. It is such a relief for him that he rushes excitedly round to see Mr. Tomb, the undertaker.

"How much to bury my wife?" asks Hamish.

"Five hundred pounds," replies Tomb, rubbing his hands together.

"Five hundred?" splutters Hamish, clutching his purse. "Can't you do it for less?"

"Well," replies Mr Tomb, "the cheapest I can manage is three hundred pounds."

"My God!" wails Hamish, counting out his money, "I almost wish she was still alive!"

Magic Mushroom Melvin, the old hippy, is busy making lunch for his old buddy, Buffalo Grass.

"Wow, man!" says Melvin, stepping back from the sink and sitting down to smoke a few reefers. "That's the wildest recipe I have ever tried."

"Groovy, man!" says Buffalo Grass, in a cloud of smoke. "What is it?"

"It is salad, man!" says Melvin.

"Hey, cool, man—salad!" agrees Buffalo Grass. "How do you make it?"

"Well, it's really easy, man!" says Melvin, "you cut up lettuce, tomatoes, cucumbers, and carrots; then you throw in some LSD, stand back, and watch the salad toss itself!"

Dilly and Dally are identical twin brothers, who live in a small town near the sea.

Dilly is married and Dally is single, but he keeps a small rowing boat.

One day Dilly's wife dies, and a few days later, Dally's rowing boat sinks.

Walking in the street a week later, Dally meets Mrs. Godball, the bishop's wife. Mrs. Godball mistakes Dally, the boatman, for Dilly, who has just lost his wife.

"I'm sorry to hear about your terrible loss!" says Mrs. Godball.

"Oh, thank you very much!" replies Dally, the boatman, "but I am not sorry at all. She was a rotten old thing from the start. She had a huge crack in the front of her and a big hole behind, which kept getting bigger every time I used her. She stank of old fish and used to leak water all the time. Her bottom was really badly scratched up, and whenever there was wind, it was not safe to go near her.

"Last week, three men came around looking for some fun, so I hired her out to them. I told them to take it easy with her, but the three idiots all tried to get into her at the same time. Of course, she split from back to front. Now she is gone, and I am very happy about it!"

Mrs. Godball faints.

Nivedano...

Nivedano...

Be silent.
Close your eyes,
and feel your body to be completely frozen.
Look inwards with absolute urgency.
Deeper and deeper,
until you reach the source of your very being.
It is very close—just one step
and you are the buddha.
Such a beautiful evening,
and the dancing rains rejoicing in your silence,
rejoicing in your samadhi.
These cloud buddhas
have come from so far away,
don't let them down.
Deeper and deeper,
there is no need to fear.
It is your own space and it is your own birthright

to be a buddha.
To make it absolutely clear
that you are not the body, nor the mind,
but just a witness,
Nivedano...

Relax, and just be a witness.
This witnessing is another name of the buddha.
Witnessing makes you an empty mirror,
reflecting everything without getting identified.
And this is the miracle of meditation;
it gives you freedom, it gives you the beyond.
Gather the experience, the fragrance,
because the time is close that you will be called back.
Taste the nectar,
the eternally running stream of your life,
let it sink deep in your every fiber,
because it is going to be a twenty-four hour lifestyle.
Living or dead, you have to remain as a buddha.
Nivedano...

Come back, but come back as a buddha
with a samadhi,
with a feel of the nectar.
Sit down for a few moments,
just to recollect the experience
of where you have been,
what you have been.
Every day it has to become deeper and deeper.

Okay, Maneesha?
Yes, Beloved Master.
Can we celebrate the buddhas?
Yes, Beloved Master.

ripe plum

Our Beloved Master,

One day, when Ma Tzu was on his way home from Chiang-si, he stopped to visit his old master, Nangaku. When Ma Tzu had burned incense and made bows to Nangaku, Nangaku gave him this verse:

> "I advise you not to go home.
> If you do, the Tao is immovable.
> And an old woman

> *next door to you*
> *will talk of your infant name."*

Ma Tzu respectfully accepted it and swore to himself never to go home, however often he might be reborn. Staying only in Chiang-si, he had disciples come to him from all parts of China.

One day a monk called Ta-mei joined a training assembly of Ma Tzu. Ta-mei asked the master: "What is buddha?"
Ma Tzu replied: "It is the present mind."
On hearing this, Ta-mei attained his full enlightenment. He took himself off into the mountains, and over the years hardly noticed the passing of time; he only saw the mountains around him turn green or yellow.
One day, Ma Tzu sent a monk especially to test him. The monk asked Ta-mei, "When you once saw Ma Tzu, by what word did you become enlightened?"
Ta-mei replied, "By Ma Tzu's saying, 'The present mind is the buddha.'"
"Now his way is another," the monk told Ta-mei.
"What is it then?" asked Ta-mei.
"Ma Tzu now says that this very mind which is buddha is neither mind nor buddha," replied the monk.
"That old fellow!" said Ta-mei. "When will he cease to confuse the minds of men? Let him go on with his 'neither mind nor buddha.' I will stick to 'this present mind itself is buddha.'"
When the messenger told Ma Tzu of this exchange, Ma Tzu commented: "The fruit of a plum has ripened."

maneesha, one of the most important things to be remembered all along is that the Zen master is not a philosopher. He is not rational. Basically he is very irrational and absurd, but miraculously he manages—from his absurdity, from his contradictory statements —to make the message clear to you. Today he may say something and tomorrow something else. If you bring your logical mind into it, you will think that you are being confused. But there are different ways of saying the same thing. In fact even in contradictions the same message can be given.

This is one of the great contributions of Zen, that there are no contradictions. Everything is expressing the same truth, the same reality. The smallest piece of grass and the biggest star are not in any way giving you a different message. Nobody is lower and nobody is higher in existence. There is no hierarchy. And as far as truth is concerned, fundamentally it is inexpressible. But if you want to express the inexpressible, then you can use even contradictory terms to indicate the same thing.

Two different fingers, coming from two different angles, can point to the same moon. The mind may find it difficult. In fact the Zen master's whole work is to make things so difficult for the mind that you become tired of the mind, tired of thinking, and you put it aside. And that moment of restfulness, when you have put the mind aside, brings you to the door of existence.

This small anecdote is very significant.

Ma Tzu stayed with his master, Nangaku, for more than ten years. On leaving him, he became abbot of the Kai-yuan Temple at Chiang-si.

In his sermons, Ma Tzu followed closely the basic insights of the sixth patriarch, Enō—particularly, that there is no buddha outside of one's own mind.

This word 'mind' can be understood as the ordinary mind, full of thoughts, emotions, sentiments and attachments. And this same mind can also be thought of as empty. You can empty it of all thoughts, of all emotions. And the moment this mind is empty, there is no difference between mind and no-mind. So there is no need to be confused.

A few masters will use: "The present mind contains everything, even the buddha." But the condition is that the mind should be empty. Then it, itself, is the buddha.

Buddha's own statement is significant. He says, "This very body, the buddha; this very mind, the lotus paradise." But continuously he is saying that you are not the body, you are not the mind. Then what does he mean with this contradiction? He is simply saying that if you are not identified with the body, this very body is as much a buddha as anything in the world. If you are not filled with thoughts, this very mind is as spacious as the whole sky. He is not contradicting himself, he is simply using contradictory ways to indicate the truth.

Enō was the man who had introduced Ma Tzu to Nangaku. Enō was getting old and Ma Tzu was very young, so he did not take the responsibility of guiding Ma Tzu into meditation. He gave the responsibility to Nangaku who was going to be his successor when he died. But the way Enō introduced Ma Tzu to Nangaku was so insightful: "Be very careful with this young man. He is going to be a buddha, and he is going to be your successor, just as you are my successor. Be very reverent, grateful, that you have got a man who is on the verge of becoming a buddha in your hands."

Ma Tzu remained closer to Enō's teachings although Enō was not his master, but Enō had seen his potentiality—the possibility, the invisible future. And at the same time he had seen that his death was coming closer, so taking on the responsibility of a disciple at this moment would be wrong, and particularly of a disciple who needs tremendous care because he is on the very verge of exploding. Being very old he thought it would be better that Ma Tzu should be given into the hands of his successor, Nangaku.

Nangaku was a master in his own right. His teaching was not just a following of Enō. In the world of Zen it is not necessary that a disciple should follow the master in details. All that is necessary is that the disciple should understand the master's presence, his fundamental realization. It should not remain a belief to the disciple, it should become an actual taste. Doctrines and beliefs don't matter at all. What matters is the master's presence and his realization, and the splendor that the realization brings with it.

Enō never asked Nangaku to follow him—Nangaku had his own approach—but he had chosen Nangaku to be his successor. This is very strange. It does not happen in any other place in the whole world. People choose successors to follow them in detail. But Zen is unique in every way. It is not a question of following, it is that this man is also realized. His methods may be different, his devices may be different, his approaches may be different, but he is a realized man, he can be a successor.

But strangely, although Enō had given the responsibility of his initiation to Nangaku, Ma Tzu remained fundamentally close to Enō's teaching, to Enō's method of indicating the truth. Enō had caught a glimpse of his future. Nangaku took every care and helped him to become an enlightened master. But he was always more grateful towards Enō for this very reason: that he had refused to initiate him, because his death was very close; and he had put him in the hands of the right person, who would take care of him, because his spring was coming soon. He would be blossoming, and Enō would not be there.

Certainly Ma Tzu and Enō, without any relationship of master and disciple, came very close in their hearts. Their hearts started beating in the same rhythm. His master's teaching was in many ways different, particularly from Enō's teaching that there is no buddha outside of one's own mind.

But remember it, when Enō says 'mind', you can translate it as 'no-mind'. What he means is 'empty mind' which is equivalent to 'no-mind'. What is left in an empty mind?—just a pure space. It depends on you whether you prefer to call it the empty mind or no-mind. But both are equivalent, not in the dictionaries, but in the existential experience.

One day, when Ma Tzu was on his way home from Chiang-si, he stopped to visit his old master, Nangaku.

He is a master now in his own right. He had gone to Chiang-si and was returning home from there, and *he stopped to visit his old master, Nangaku. When Ma Tzu had burned incense and made bows to Nangaku, Nangaku gave him this verse....*

This too has to be understood. Even when a disciple becomes enlightened, it does not matter, his gratefulness becomes even fuller. It is not that now there is no need of the master. It is not that "Now I am equal to the master, now I am experiencing the same buddhahood as the master." No, it is not thought of in that way, because that is the way of the ego. The ego has been lost long ago. The way of gratitude, the way of humbleness is that "Though I may have become a buddha, my master was the indicator towards the right path, and I will remain forever and forever in deep gratitude towards him."

Sariputta, one of Buddha's chief disciples, became enlightened. With tears in his eyes he came to Buddha and he said, "I was avoiding enlightenment, but you went on insisting. Now I am enlightened and my eyes are full of tears because I know you will send me away from you, just to spread the fire. And I understand your compassion, that you are continuously aware of the many who can become buddhas; just a little support is needed. Those who have not gone very far away from themselves can be called back very easily."

Buddha said, "Then why are you crying?"

He said, "I am crying because I will not be able to touch your feet every day as I have been doing for these twenty years."

Buddha said, "Do one thing. Keep a map with you, and remember in what direction I am dwelling. Just bow down in that direction. Touch the feet symbolically, touch the earth—because after all this body is made of earth, and one day it will go back to the earth. So touching the earth is not only touching my feet, but touching the feet of all the buddhas who have ever happened. They have all dissolved their bodies in the earth. So there is no need, and it does not look right, that an enlightened person should weep and cry."

Sariputta said, "I don't care what people think, but the reality is that tears are coming. And according to your teachings, I should be spontaneous and authentic. Even if you say, 'Don't weep,' I am not going to listen. Tears are coming, what can I do? I cannot be a hypocrite, smiling though the eyes are full of tears."

It is said that Sariputta, wherever he was, in the morning would look at the map, to find exactly where Buddha was, and in that direction he would bow down and touch the feet of Buddha. He came to have thousands of disciples of his own and they said, "It does not look right. You need not do such a gesture. You are a buddha yourself."

He said, "It is true, I am a buddha myself, but I would not have been a buddha if I had not met Gautam the Buddha. It is the meeting with this man that triggered something in me, burned all that was false and brought all that was true in its pristine purity and clarity. I owe so much to this man that there is no way to pay him. All that I can do is touch his feet from miles away."

He continued to his very last breath. Before he died—he died before Gautam Buddha—the last thing he said to his disciples was, "Forgive me because you cannot see those invisible feet. Let me touch the feet of my master for the last time." And he bowed down, tears flowing from his eyes, and he died in that posture. He did not get up again. This is true humanity—humbleness, devotion, love, trust.

Ma Tzu, visiting his old master, burned incense in front of him as you burn incense before a buddha statue and made bows to Nangaku. Nangaku gave him this *gatha*, this verse:

"I advise you not to go home.
If you do, the Tao is immovable.
And an old woman next door to you
will talk of your infant name."

Ma Tzu respectfully accepted it and swore to himself never to go home, however often he might be reborn. Staying only in Chiang-si, he had disciples come to him from all parts of China.

Very strange but meaningful advice. Nangaku told him not to go home. It implies many things. It implies that now you are homeless. The moment you become enlightened you don't have a home, not even your body is your home. Now the whole existence is your home, so stop this old habit of going home once in a while. There is no home for you anymore. You are a homeless cloud floating in the sky, in total freedom, unattached to anything.

If you do, the Tao is immovable.

Nangaku is saying, "If you don't listen to my advice and still go home, remember that your Tao, your empty buddha inside, never goes anywhere. So you are just acting; just a dead body, a corpse is going. Your real being is immovable; it never goes anywhere, it is always now and here." And he said, *"And an old woman next door to you will talk of your infant name."*

Ma Tzu's childhood name was Baso. Nangaku is making a joke about his name, that the old woman next door to his home will call him Baso. They will not recognize that he is no more Baso, that he is Ma Tzu, that he is a great master. In their eyes he will be just the same; they have seen him born, and they have seen him growing up. It is very difficult for them to recognize that he has become a buddha, and they will think it very insulting to the Buddha.

Ma Tzu respectfully accepted it and swore to himself never to go home, however often he might be reborn.

He is saying that even if he is born again—although an enlightened person is never born again—he is giving his promise that even if he is born again and again, he will never go home. He has understood his homelessness, his aloneness.

Staying only in Chiang-si, he had disciples come to him from all parts of China.

One day a monk called Ta-mei joined a training assembly of Ma Tzu.

Ta-mei asked the master: "What is buddha?"

Ma Tzu replied: "It is the present mind"—the teaching of Enō that he followed all his life.

But remember that the mind is never in the present; it is either in the past or in the future. In the present is empty mind. You can call it the present mind if you are interested in using the positive words or you can call it no-mind, if you want to use the negative. The truth can be expressed both ways, negatively or positively. The present mind in fact means no-mind. For those who understand the presentness, all mind disappears. Mind can be in the past, mind can be in the future, but never in the present. Hence being in the present simply means being out of the grip of the mind.

Ma Tzu replied: "It is the present mind."

On hearing this, Ta-mei attained his full enlightenment. He took himself off into the mountains, and over the years hardly noticed the passing of time; he only saw the mountains around him turn green or yellow.

One day, Ma Tzu sent a monk specially to test him. The monk asked Ta-mei, "When you once saw Ma Tzu, by what word did you become enlightened?"

Ta-mei replied, "By Ma Tzu's saying, 'The present mind is the buddha.'"

"Now his way is another," the monk told Ta-mei.

"What is it then?" asked Ta-mei.

"Ma Tzu now says that this very mind which is buddha is neither mind nor buddha," replied the monk.

This very mind is neither the buddha nor the mind. Now Ma Tzu is teaching this way.

"That old fellow!" said Ta-mei. "When will he cease to confuse the

*minds of men? Let him go on with his 'neither mind nor buddha.' I will
stick to 'this present mind itself is buddha.'"*

He has understood clearly that Ma Tzu has changed his expression from positive to the negative. He can confuse an ordinary man, but he cannot confuse an enlightened man anymore.

"That old fellow!" said Ta-mei. "When will he cease to confuse the minds of men?"

There was no need to change, the old expression was perfect.

"Let him go on with his 'neither mind nor buddha.' I will stick to 'this present mind itself is buddha.'"

You may think that he is not agreeing with his master, Ma Tzu, but then you will not have understood it. He is agreeing perfectly well. He understands that it means the same. He has just changed the expression from positive to negative. Only the expression is changed, not the expressed. So he says, "Let the old fellow do whatever he wants, but I am going to insist that this present mind itself is the buddha."

When the messenger told Ma Tzu of this exchange, Ma Tzu commented: "The fruit of a plum has ripened."

Ma Tzu understood perfectly well that Ta-mei had become enlightened. Any unenlightened man would have been confused because the unenlightened mind can never think that positive and negative can be of the same significance and have the same meaning. There is a place where yes and no are not contradictory.

Ma Tzu said, "The fruit of a plum has ripened."

Ta-mei's name, in Chinese, means 'big plum'.

Takuan wrote:

*The moon has no intent to cast
its shadow anywhere,
nor does the pond design to
lodge the moon.
How serene the water of Hirosawa!*

Takuan's monastery was near the lake Hirosawa. In this small poem is contained the whole essence of Zen. *The moon has no intent to cast its shadow anywhere....*

Do you think the moon has any intention to cast its shadow and reflection into thousands of seas and lakes and ponds? It has no intent at all.

And on the other side, *nor does the pond design to lodge the moon*.

Neither the pond, the lake or the ocean are desiring to lodge the moon, or are interested to reflect the moon.

How serene the water of Hirosawa!

It is not even disturbed by the reflection of the moon. It does not care. His poem is saying to you to live without intentions, without any goals, without any desire of achievement, any ambition. Just live spontaneously, moment to moment. Whatever happens, accept it joyfully, rejoicingly, without any complaint or grudge.

Even if death comes, let it be welcomed. Dance, sing a song. That has been the tradition in Zen. Each master is expected—and they all have done it—that before dying they should write a small haiku containing their whole teaching.

It shows two things: that they are perfectly aware of death, and that even in death they are not in any sadness. Their haiku says their joy, their fulfillment. Without your asking for anything, existence has given everything to you.

A man who lives with intentions is bound to feel frustration. A man who lives with expectations is bound to feel frustrated because existence has no obligation to you. But if you live without intentions, without expectations, then miraculously you find that everything that you ever dreamed of is being fulfilled. The moon is reflected in the lake—the lake never asked it, the moon never intended it. Existence goes on spontaneously. Don't bring your desire, your ambition and your expectation; they are the disturbing points. They create a chaos in your mind. But if there is no intention for anything, *How serene the water of Hirosawa!*

The moon is reflected but the water is not even thrilled. Such a beautiful moon and the Hirosawa lake takes the reflection naturally, spontaneously. If it was not reflected, there would not have been any frustration. Moon or no moon, nothing matters. The lake of Hirosawa is silent. And that should be your inner consciousness— just a silent lake.

Maneesha has asked:

Our Beloved Master,
How amazing it would be if You turned up one evening in Gautam the
Buddha Auditorium, and all You could see was a vast hall of empty
mirrors, or rows and rows of juicy, ripe plums.
Do You really think it's possible? Is anything happening? Or better: Is
nothing *happening?*

Maneesha, it is happening every day. The whole hall is full of
mirrors and full of big plums. Look at Avirbhava, a dancing plum.
Now it has come to the point of laughter and Sardar Gurudayal
Singh is sitting very close today. Now this is a series dedicated to him.

Luscious Miss Willing is having trouble sleeping. Her dreams and
her reality are so full of sexual activity that she cannot tell what is
real and what is not. So she goes to see Doctor Feelgood for profes-
sional help.
It is her first visit, so Feelgood hears her problem, then starts
yakkety-yakking about all kinds of Freudian sexual terminology.
"Wait a minute," interrupts Miss Willing. "What is a phallic
symbol?"
"A phallic symbol," explains Feelgood, "represents the phallus."
"Okay," says the girl, "what is a phallus?"
"I guess," says Feelgood, a grin on his face, "the best way to
explain it is to show you." So Feelgood stands up, unzips his pants,
and pulls out his machinery.
"This, young lady," says Feelgood, proudly, "is a phallus!"
"Oh!" says Miss Willing, smiling. "You mean it is like a prick,
only smaller!"

The aging, dilapidated president, Ronald Reagan, is waiting to
board the official presidential plane that is taking him to Europe.
His personal secretary Reginald, who has come to see him off,
leans up to Ronnie and whispers, "What's your advice on the Homo-
sexual Bill?"

"Oh, yes," says Reagan. "Tell him that I'll pay him when I get back!"

"I don't see you at the gang-bangs any more," says Marvyn, the Hell's Angel, to his old friend, Pigpen. "What happened?"

"I got married," says Pigpen.

"No shit, man!" says Marvyn. "Is legalized screwing any better than the regular kind?"

"It is not even so good," replies Pigpen, "but at least you don't have to stand in line for it!"

Fergus and Funky are lost in the baking deserts of the burning Sahara. They have been crawling on their hands and knees for days, in search of water. Almost at the end of their rope, they suddenly spot a man in the distance with a small stand, selling something.

Fergus and Funky struggle and crawl their way up to the man, and with their tongues hanging out they shout, "Water! Please give us water!"

"Sorry, fellas," says the man, "I'd love to, but I don't have any water. I'm selling neckties. Got some beauties if you'd like a sharp-looking tie!"

"Neckties?" screams Funky, and he faints.

"No," says Fergus, "we don't want any goddam ties—we need water!"

And the two thirsty men drag themselves on.

Three days later, off in the distance, a large building appears on the horizon. Inspired, the worn-out duo drag themselves up to it. It is the very exclusive Screwing Sands Hotel.

Fergus crawls up to the doorman, who is standing stiffly in his three-piece uniform.

"Water!" cries Fergus, with his parched lips quivering. "We need to come in and get water!"

"I am sorry, sir," replies the doorman. "But I am afraid you cannot enter without a tie!"

Nivedano...

Nivedano…

Be silent. Close your eyes.
Feel the body to be completely frozen.
Look inwards as deeply as possible.
This is the way.
At the very end of the way, you are the buddha.
And the journey is very short—a single step.
Just total urgency and absolute honesty is needed
to look straight into your own being.
There is the mirror we have been talking about.

The mirror is the buddha.
It is your eternal nature.
Deeper and deeper.
You have to go in until you find yourself.
Don't hesitate.
There is no fear.
Of course you are alone,
but this aloneness is a great, beautiful experience.
And on this path you will not meet anyone
except yourself.
To make it clear that you are just a mirror,
a witness of your body, of your mind, of everything,
Nivedano…

Relax,
and just be a watchful, witnessing mirror,
reflecting everything.
Neither do those things have any intentions
to be reflected,
nor do you have any intention
to catch their reflections.
Just be a silent lake of Hirosawa,
and all bliss is yours,
and this evening becomes a benediction.
This present moment becomes no-mind, no-time,
just a purity, a space unbounded.
This is your freedom.
And unless you are a buddha, you are not free.
You know nothing of freedom.

Let this experience sink deep
in every fiber of your being.
Get soaked, drenched.
When you come back, come back drenched
with the mist of your buddha nature.
And remember this space, this way,
because you have to carry it out twenty-four hours
in all your actions.
Sitting, standing, walking, sleeping,
you have to remain a buddha.
Then the whole existence becomes an ecstasy.
Nivedano…

Come back,
but bring with you all the experience,
slowly, silently, gracefully.
Sit down for a few moments,
recollecting the place you have been to,
remembering the joy and the silence
of being just a mirror,
the immense freedom that comes
when you are just a mirror
unattached to anything, homeless, alone.
You become an Everest of consciousness.

Okay, Maneesha?
Yes, Beloved Master.
Can we celebrate the ten thousand buddhas?
Yes, Beloved Master.

twisted nose

Our Beloved Master,

One day, as Hyakujō was visiting his master, Ma Tzu, a flock of wild geese flew overhead. Ma Tzu asked, "What are they?"

"They are wild geese, sir," said Hyakujō.

"Where are they?" asked the master.

"They have flown away, sir," replied Hyakujō.

Ma Tzu suddenly took hold of Hyakujō's nose and twisted it. Overcome

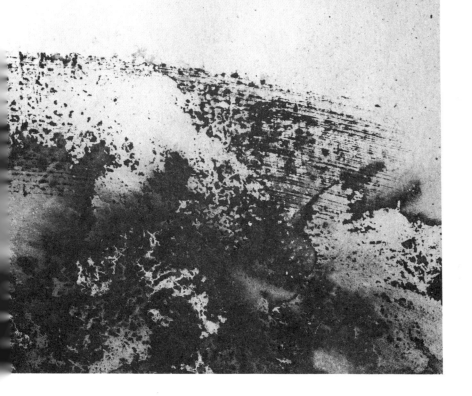

with pain, Hyakujō cried out. Ma Tzu said, "You say they have flown away, but all the same they have been here from the very beginning."

At that moment, Hyakujō attained enlightenment.

The next day, at a regular assembly, Ma Tzu had hardly sat down when Hyakujō came to roll up his mat, which made the master descend from the platform. Hyakujō followed him into his room.

Ma Tzu said, "Just now, before I had begun my sermon, what made you roll up my mat?"

Hyakujō said, "Yesterday your reverence twisted my nose and I felt acute pain."

"Where did you apply your mind yesterday?" Ma Tzu asked.

All that the disciple said was, "I feel no more pain in the nose today."

Thereupon the master commented, "You have profoundly understood yesterday's episode."

On another occasion, as soon as Ma Tzu sat down on the Zazen bench as usual, he spat.

A monk asked, "Why did you spit?"

Ma Tzu said, "When I sat here, there were mountains, rivers, and the whole natural universe in front of me. I spat because I didn't like that."

The monk said, "But the universe is so splendid! Why don't you like that?"

Ma Tzu replied, "It may be splendid to you, but it is disgusting to me."

The monk continued, "What kind of mental state is this?"

Ma Tzu said, "This is the state of a bodhisattva."

Maneesha, these are some of the great episodes in the history of Zen. They show your realization in your action. When a master acts in a certain way, the disciple spontaneously has to respond, not through thinking, but through his very empty heart.

Zen is ultimately a device, thousands of devices, created by different masters to provoke awakening in you. Reading them one may think they are just anecdotes, stories, puzzles. They are not, they are communications, and communications of the greatest value.

One day, as Hyakujō was visiting his master, Ma Tzu, a flock of wild

geese flew overhead. Ma Tzu asked, "What are they?"
"They are wild geese, sir," said Hyakujō.
"Where are they?" asked the master.
"They have flown away, sir," replied Hyakujō.
Ma Tzu suddenly took hold of Hyakujō's nose and twisted it.
Overcome with pain, Hyakujō cried out. Ma Tzu said, "You say they have flown away, but all the same they have been here from the very beginning."
At that moment, Hyakujō attained enlightenment.

To any ordinary rational thinker this will look like an absurd statement. But to a man attuned in meditation, this can become a tremendous awakening point. It is not that Ma Tzu does not know that the geese have flown away. It is not that he does not know that the geese were there. He is not asking for any knowledgeable answer. He is asking for the response which Hyakujō missed in the beginning, when Ma Tzu asked him, *"What are they?"* Obviously Ma Tzu knows what they are.

So remember, it is not a question or inquiry about knowing the object. At this point Hyakujō missed. His response was through the mind; he said, *"They are wild geese, sir."*

That would be the response of anybody else in the whole world. It is not out of the empty heart. It is not out of the mirror of nothingness. It is just...any child would say it. The answer is right, but Hyakujō's response was not through the heart, it was through the mind.

"They are wild geese, sir," said Hyakujō.

Here he missed. He should have responded to the question without thinking of any consequences.

"Where are they?"—the master gave him another chance—*asked the master.*

"They have flown away, sir," replied Hyakujō.

He is just functioning on the mental level.

Ma Tzu suddenly took hold of Hyakujō's nose and twisted it.

Overcome with pain, Hyakujō cried out. Ma Tzu said, "You say they have flown away, but all the same they have been here from the very beginning."

Where can they go? They have always been here and will be here. The here is vast enough—wherever they are, they are in the here. They cannot go out of the here. That's what he was expecting from Hyakujō. But he had to take Hyakujō by his nose and twist the nose to make him aware that he was functioning through the mind. And the mind can only bring pain; the mind *is* pain.

Ma Tzu's twisting the nose of Hyakujō and giving him tremendous pain so that he cried out—don't take it superficially, don't take it as it appears on the surface. This crying out was not out of the mind. This crying out came as the spontaneous response of his whole being. At this moment the master could speak to him. He was in the right space now; he was no more in the mind, his whole being was awake because of the pain.

Pain has a tremendous value in awakening. Pain has been used by many masters to awaken the sleeping disciple. All your old religions, on the contrary, console the disciple and help him to sleep well —God is in heaven and everything is okay on the earth, you don't be worried! But Zen is not at all interested in consoling you. It is interested in awakening you.

When Hyakujō cried out, Ma Tzu did not say a single word of sympathy. He did not give any explanation, why he had twisted his nose. On the contrary he said, *"You say they have flown away, but all the same they have been here from the very beginning."*

In that moment there was no thought except pain. The mind was empty, the nose was hurting—and Ma Tzu did not care about the nose or the pain; he simply stated a tremendously meaningful statement, that nobody, nothing, can go away out of here. Here is immense and vast, so is now. Wherever they are, they are here.

Hyakujō was now in a right state to understand the meaning of the master—that everything is always here. Those wild geese were just an excuse to explain to Hyakujō that nothing moves, nothing goes anywhere.

At that moment Hyakujō attained enlightenment.

Seeing the point, the eternity and the wideness of now and here, he immediately fell into the emptiness of his heart and realized the truth. In an instant something was triggered in him by what Ma Tzu was saying, which Zen calls enlightenment. He became aware of his own hereness, of his own nowness. The wild geese were just an excuse.

But such anecdotes have never happened anywhere else. They have no parallel, hence the difficulty of understanding them. They are anecdotes on the path of meditation. Only people of the path who have gone deep into meditation will be able to understand something which looks absolutely absurd as far as reason is concerned.

The nose has nothing to do with attainment, otherwise it would be very easy. The disciple simply comes, gets a twisted nose, becomes enlightened and goes home. And Ma Tzu would not twist the nose of any disciple, any XYZ.

Hyakujō is ready. It is just a push. He is just on the boundary line, where anything can push him just that one single step inwards. It is such a great statement, that there is no time and there is no space— here is the only space and now is the only time.

And it is not applicable only to the wild geese, it is applicable to you, to everything—the great statement and the silent watchfulness. Awakened by the twisted nose, Hyakujō attained enlightenment.

The next day, at a regular assembly, Ma Tzu had hardly sat down when Hyakujō came to roll up his mat, which made the master descend from the platform. Hyakujō followed him into his room.
Ma Tzu said, "Just now, before I had begun my sermon, what made you roll up my mat?"
Hyakujō said, "Yesterday your reverence twisted my nose and I felt acute pain."
"Where did you apply your mind yesterday?" Ma Tzu asked.
All that the disciple said was, "I feel no more pain in the nose today."
Thereupon the master commented, "You have profoundly understood yesterday's episode."

This is a little more subtle than the first episode. Usually the Zen master gives the sermon and the chief disciple, when the sermon is over, rolls up the mat on which he was sitting and takes the mat to his room. But in this case *Hyakujō came to roll up his mat, which made the master descend from the platform. Hyakujō followed him into his room.*

He has not even uttered a single word. Hyakujō has become an enlightened master himself. Yesterday's experience... Now he is responding the way a master responds; he is saying, by rolling up the mat, "Now I don't need any sermon. All I needed, I got yesterday."

Ma Tzu said, "Just now, before I had begun my sermon, what made you roll up my mat?"

Hyakujō said, "Yesterday your reverence twisted my nose and I felt acute pain."

"Where did you apply your mind yesterday?"

"Could you not have done something yesterday?" Ma Tzu is asking. *All that the disciple said was, "I feel no more pain in the nose today."*

He is saying, "I don't need any consolation. I feel no pain in the nose today and I don't need any sermon anymore. You said everything yesterday."

Thereupon the master commented, "You have profoundly understood yesterday's episode."

On another occasion, as soon as Ma Tzu sat down on the Zazen bench as usual, he spat.

A monk asked, "Why did you spit?"

Ma Tzu said, "When I sat here, there were mountains, rivers, and the whole natural universe in front of me. I spat because I didn't like that."

The monk said, "But the universe is so splendid! Why don't you like that?"

Ma Tzu replied, "It may be splendid to you, but it is disgusting to me."

The monk continued, "What kind of mental state is this?"

Ma Tzu said, "This is the state of a bodhisattva."

This, the third part of the anecdote, is even more difficult to understand. Ma Tzu, spitting on the Zazen bench, is not really saying that he doesn't like the mountains and the rivers and the stars. What he is doing is seeing whether the disciple remains silent and non-judgmental, or makes a judgment.

Zen's whole attitude is non-judgmental. Don't judge...and at least the disciple should not judge the action of his master, he should simply witness, he should simply see that Ma Tzu has spat. Ma Tzu is provoking him; he is provoking his judgmental mind. And the monk has forgotten that the whole teaching is to never judge. Just watch, and particularly watch the actions of the master. Do you think that Ma Tzu does not understand that spitting on the bench is simply disgusting? But he wants you to remain unwavering, non-judgmental, just watching, as a mirror.

If a mirror was watching, do you think the mirror would say "What are you doing? This is not good." The disciple missed; this could have been a great opportunity to become enlightened. Remember it, devices don't succeed all the time. Sometimes they fail.

The master makes his wholehearted effort but the disciple may not be in the right space to understand it. Now it is very clear to a man of a little meditation that Ma Tzu knows that spitting on the Zazen bench is disgusting, so there is no need to ask any question. Perhaps he is provoking you, he is provoking your judgmental mind. And the moment the judgmental mind comes in, your watching mind disappears. Remember these two words—judgmental and watching. You can watch only if you don't judge.

But the disciple could not resist asking. He asked, *"Why did you spit?"* He forgot completely that here he has to learn watching, not making judgments, particularly of any action of the master.

Ma Tzu said, "When I sat here, there were mountains, rivers, and the whole natural universe in front of me. I spat because I didn't like that."

Still the disciple could not understand that there were no mountains, no rivers, no universe there in front of the Zazen bench; the master's explanation is just to test him.

He said, *"I spat because I didn't like that."*

A meditative disciple would have slapped Ma Tzu, he would not have asked anything, and that would have been greatly appreciated by Ma Tzu. That would have been the disciple's enlightenment. It is not a question of asking, it is a question of responding. The master obviously is doing something wrong, just to provoke. If the disciple had slapped the master without saying anything, the master would have laughed and blessed the disciple, saying, "You have understood it." But because the disciple missed the point, he again said, *"I spat because I didn't like that."*

He wants the disciple to say to him, "What happened to your

non-judgmental mind?" But the disciple had forgotten completely about the non-judgmental mind, which is the very foundation of Zen.

The monk said, "But the universe is so splendid!"

He started arguing. With the master you don't argue, you respond. You don't start a verbal conversation—that will be missing the master and his great compassion.

The monk said, "But the universe is so splendid! Why don't you like that?"

He has come down to the level of the mind and is on the point of discussing the matter. But Zen does not allow discussion. It is not a debate. It is pure awakening from the mind, pure freedom from judgment.

Ma Tzu replied, "It may be splendid to you, but it is disgusting to me."

He is again and again trying to remind the disciple that he should slap him for being judgmental, that he has completely forgotten the foundation.

The monk continued, "What kind of mental state is this?"

He is continuing on the mental state.

Ma Tzu said, "This is the state of a bodhisattva."

This is the state of a buddha. Now there is nothing else to be said. Ma Tzu has closed the conversation, seeing that the device has failed.

So remember that a device will not always succeed, because there are two persons involved—the master who is enlightened, and the disciple who is not enlightened. And he will most probably behave in an unenlightened way, not knowing that this is the time to act spontaneously, not through the mind, but through the empty heart.

Daiō wrote in praise of Kannon:

The cliffs are high and deep,
the waters rush and tumble.
The realm of perfect communion
is new in each place.
Face to face, the people who
meet her don't recognize her.
When will they ever be free from
the harbor of illusion?

Each moment in existence is a moment ready for communion. There is no special moment in which you can become enlightened. Every moment is special. Every moment is potential for your enlightenment—a beautiful sunset, a beautiful sunrise, a great sky full of stars, or just this silence. Anything will do, if you remember yourself to be a watcher—not getting involved, not getting identified, but just remaining a mirror, an empty mirror.

Before the empty mirror no illusion can remain for long. All illusions will disappear; they remain only because you get involved with them.

Daiō is asking with great compassion, *When will they ever be free from the harbor of illusion?*

Every moment the time comes for enlightenment. Every moment is the right season, the right climate; you just go on missing. Missing becomes your habit, and that habit has to be broken. You have to become stabilized, concentrated in the moment, at the center of your being; just watching without saying a single word of evaluation, good, bad or beautiful.

Nothing has to be said, just watching is enough and all illusions disappear, all that is false disappears.

Maneesha has asked:

Our Beloved Master,
The story about Ma Tzu spitting brought home to me how everything You do and say seems to be only for Your disciples' sake.
You relate to such a diverse bunch of us—from dancing plums to hot potatoes, from German stoneheads to laughing sardarjis—and yet You are never other than Yourself, just like water that takes the shape of whatever container it flows into and yet doesn't lose its essential nature.
Is it that when You are nobody, You can be anybody?

Maneesha, when you are nobody, you are already everybody. Nobody and everybody mean the same thing. And my calling some of you hot potatoes or dancing plums, German stoneheads or laughing sardarjis—they are all devices. And I know that you are in the right place and you will not misunderstand me. It is out of love and out of compassion that I call you any name. For example, I called Avirbhava a big ripe plum. She understood it. She waved me a kiss. And today she is sitting there, hiding an egg.

Avirbhava, bring your egg here...bring it.

(Avirbhava puts a big green egg in front of the Master, on the podium. She breaks it, and two baby chicks jump out and hop around while the Master chuckles.)

Yeah, that is the right egg!

Now the time for Sardarji has come. He is sitting exactly in the first row. From the very last row he has come to the first.

Paddy is in a dark mood, so he goes to see the famous channeler, Madam Hippo.

"Ah," says the woman, staring into her crystal ball, "the signs are not good."

"Really?" says Paddy, wide-eyed. "What does it say?"

"Well," she intones, "it says that you will be a widower in one week!"

Paddy wipes the sweat from his face and leans back.

"I know that!" he says. "What I want to know is—will I get caught?"

George Bush, the American vice president, telephones the Justice Department at three o'clock in the morning. He insists that he must speak to the chief justice immediately.

Finally, the housekeeper decides to wake him up.

"Well, what is it?" demands the chief justice.

"Your honor," exclaims Bush, "Ronald and Nancy Reagan have just taken poison together in the White House underground bunker, and they are both dead!"

"Really?" says the judge, yawning.

"Yes, really!" cries Bush. "The undertaker is here already to put them in their coffins."

"Really?" says the sleepy judge.

"Yes, really!" shouts Bush, "and since I'm the vice president, I want to take Reagan's place!"

"Well, it's okay with me," replies the judge, "if it's okay with the undertaker!"

Walter and Peggy Sue are out on a date together in Walter's new Ford Thunderbird. He is going so slowly that it is driving Peggy Sue bananas.

"Listen," says Peggy Sue, excitedly, "every time you speed up the car ten miles per hour, I will take off a piece of my clothing!"

Walter immediately puts his foot down on the accelerator, and off come her shoes. Walter smiles, pushes on the gas, and off comes her blouse. Walter's eyes bulge out, he stomps the pedal to the floor, and off come Peggy Sue's bra, skirt, and finally, her lace panties.

Walter gets so excited that he gets his machinery stuck in the steering wheel and loses control of the car. It skids off the road, and rolls over. Neither of them are hurt, but Walter is stuck underneath the car.

"Quick!" pants Walter. "Go for help!"

Frantic and stark naked, Peggy Sue starts running around in all directions. She picks up one of Walter's shoes, holds it over her pussy, and runs to the nearest garage.

There she bumps into big Rufus, the black guy, as he is fixing a car.

"You have got to help!" Peggy Sue explains breathlessly to Rufus. "My boyfriend is stuck!"

Rufus looks at the girl for a long minute.

"Lady," he replies slowly, "if he's up that far, we'll never get him out!"

Nivedano...

Nivedano...

Be silent.
Close your eyes.
Feel the body to be completely frozen.
Go inwards with your total energy,
with a great urgency,
as if this is the last moment of your life
and you have to reach to the center
and the source of your being.
Deeper and deeper,
your life center is also
the center of the whole universe.
It is from your life center
that you are nourished by existence.
Just watch the silence,
the peace,
the immense splendor
of your being.
You are the buddha
when you are watching;

64

the same mind when empty becomes the buddha.
The buddha is nothing but an empty mirror—
no judgment,
just a watchfulness,
a witnessing,
and you have arrived.
To make it more clear,
Nivedano...

Relax.
Let go of the body, of the mind;
leave them and just be a watcher.
The body is not you,
the mind is not you,
you are only a pure witness.
This is your buddhahood.
Rejoice in it.
Get soaked and drenched in the blessing
that spontaneously showers
at the center of your being.
This center of your being has to become
your circumference also.
Slowly, slowly
you have to bring the buddha out
in your actions, in your words,
in your silences.
Day in, day out, the buddha has to become
just your heartbeat.
This immensely beautiful evening

has become even more beautiful,
with ten thousand buddhas just watching.
The eternity of existence,
like the wild geese,
is always here.
You have never been anywhere else.
You have always been here and now.
Remember it.
When you come back,
bring that remembrance with you.
It has to become your very life,
your very character.

Nivedano…

Come back, but bring the buddha with you.
Come back as an empty mirror
and sit down for few seconds as a buddha—
remembering, recollecting
the great experience you have passed through.

Okay, Maneesha?
Yes, Beloved Master.
Can we celebrate the ten thousand buddhas?
Yes, Beloved Master.

Our Beloved Master,

Ma Tzu had three outstanding disciples who enjoyed a special intimacy with him. They were Nan-chuan, Chih-tsang, and Hui-hai (otherwise known as Hyakujō).

One evening, as the three disciples were attending on their master, enjoying the moon together, he asked them what they thought would be the best way of spending such a night.

like a cow

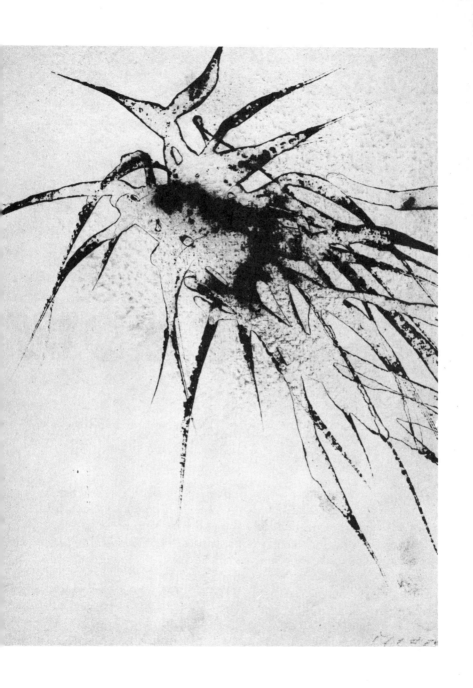

Chih-tsang was the first to answer. He said, "A good time to make offerings."
Hui-hai said, "A good time to cultivate one's spiritual life."
Nan-chuan made no answer, but shook his sleeves and went away.
Ma Tzu turned to Chih-tsang and said, "The sutras will join the tsang."
(He was making a pun on Chih-tsang's name, tsang, which in Chinese means 'basket', as in carrying the word of Buddha.)
He turned toward Hui-hai and said: "Dhyana will return to the sea."
(Ma Tzu was making a second pun, since, in Chinese, hai means 'sea'.)
Then Ma Tzu concluded, "Nan-chuan alone transcends the realm of all things, all by himself."

On another occasion a monk asked Ma Tzu, "What is the Buddha?"
Ma Tzu answered, "Mind is the Buddha."
The monk then asked, "What is the Way?"
"No-mind is the Way," answered Ma Tzu.
The monk then asked, "Are the Buddha and the Way somewhat different?"
Ma Tzu replied, "The Buddha is like stretching out the hand, the Way is like clenching the fist."

maneesha, before entering the sutras something has to be said about Ma Tzu himself, because it is very strange... No other Zen master has ever behaved the way Ma Tzu behaved—but it is very symbolic.
Ma Tzu is said to have been a strange-looking man. It is said that he walked like a cow, and looked around like a tiger. He could touch his nose with his tongue, and had two rings on the soles of his feet.
Ma Tzu's way of teaching was most varied. He is said to have been instrumental in the enlightenment of one hundred and thirty disciples, each of whom became the master of a particular locality.
Obviously this strange man, Ma Tzu, behaved according to his spontaneity, not caring about anybody in the world. That is the first thing to be understood. Only a man of tremendous courage can walk on all fours like a cow—a man who does not care a bit about the

opinions of others. He knows the truth and that is the end.

And walking like a cow is very symbolic. You cannot fall asleep standing up, it is very difficult. You have to lie down horizontally, so that the gravitational pull is equal all over the body. Standing, leaning or sitting, the gravitational pull will be different on different parts of the body. That is a disturbance in your harmoniousness. But when you lie down you come into a deep harmony with the gravitational field.

There is a strange story in Zen circles—it is very ancient—that animals know our language perfectly well, but they don't speak, they don't show even a sign that they understand us.

Once a Zen master said to a monkey—only a Zen master can do such a thing—"I know it perfectly well; my insight says that you understand my language but you are trying to hide the fact."

The monkey said, "Yes, sir. But please don't tell anybody because I will not speak in front of anybody else. So keep it a secret. Every animal understands your language, but no animal wants to be enslaved by you. The moment any animal speaks, he is going to be put to do some work."

That ancient story reminded me of a child who never spoke until he was eight years old. Every effort was made, every test was made; his ears were perfect, there was no defect as far as physiology was concerned. It was a mystery why he did not respond. Finally they took him to a psychiatrist, but to no avail.

One day he shouted at his mother, "Mummy, where is the salt?" He was taking his lunch. The mother could not believe it, and she was alone in the house, nobody would believe her. For eight years the child had been defying.

The mother asked him, "Why have you been silent for eight years?"

He said, "Everything was perfect until now. Just today the salt is missing. There was no need to speak before. Why bother?"

But she said, "Will you speak in front of others?"

He refused. He said, "This is just a secret between us. Don't tell anybody, otherwise you will be thought to be lying. I will keep my silence again."

What is the reason why animals don't speak and why they don't grow their minds, their intelligence; why they are so contented, like a cow? It is because they are horizontal. There is no disturbance. In their physiology, in their psychology, everything is balanced. Gravitation is not disturbed. Man, by standing up on his two legs, has disturbed the whole balance. And his head started growing just because he was standing up.

It is a scientific fact that man's standing on two legs is the cause of his increasing intelligence. Mind, in a small head, is a very complicated phenomenon; one billion small nerves make it, and those small nerves are almost invisible. They need a very small quantity of oxygen in the blood. Just a little more blood and it is almost like a flood—just as in Bangladesh, right now, three fourths of Bangladesh is taken over by water. Animals have not grown their brain, their mind, because the flood of blood to every part is equal.

Since man is standing up, it is very difficult for his heart, for his lungs, because it is going against gravitation to send oxygen and blood to the brain. The quantity became so small that this was the reason that man could grow very subtle nerves which can think, which can philosophize, which can even transcend thinking, which can make one a buddha.

Ma Tzu's habit of walking on all fours just like a cow... The first implication is that he is now a no-mind, just as all animals are; that he has joined the world and dropped his mind; that he is now in tune with the universe, not struggling against it but just floating with it. The second implication is that because he has dropped the mind, he has become an emptiness—and it automatically grows into compassion, into love, into humbleness, into egolessness. You cannot find another animal like the cow in its humbleness, simplicity, contentment—and yet he looked around like a tiger.

That is the contradiction of Zen. You should be like a cow, utterly humble, but you should be as rebellious and revolutionary and radical as a tiger. So although he walked like a cow, you could see that his eyes were those of a tiger—he would jump on you and finish you! Whether it is symbolic or actual is very difficult to decide. But the contemporary sources all say that it is true.

He walked like a cow, and looked around like a tiger. He could touch his nose with his tongue. Very rare people can do it. Only very rare people can move their earlobes. Try to move your earlobes. They are yours but absolutely out of your control—you have no control over them.

I have come across only one man, a doctor in my village, and he was a student with me in the school and in the university. He is the only man in the whole world, perhaps, who can move his earlobes according to his will. It is a miracle to see how he manages it, because it is an impossibility if the earlobes are natural. They don't have any nervous system, so you cannot manage them. You need a certain nervous system that can be controlled by the mind. But there is no nervous system, it is just pure flesh.

Perhaps this doctor—his name is Manohar—has got, by some mistake of nature, a nervous system in his earlobes. There is no other explanation. In China it is ancient lore that you cannot touch your nose with your tongue. But near to your death, you can touch it. The simple reason is that your teeth have fallen out—it is nothing miraculous—and so the nose and the tongue have come closer.

In India a similar kind of idea has been prevalent, which is more significant. Six months before your death you stop being able to see the tip of your nose because your eyes start rolling up. The moment you cannot see the tip, you can be certain that within six months you will be dead, because the eyes have started moving upwards. That's why, when somebody dies, you immediately close his eyes. Because to see him...just the white of the eyes is showing, the black part has turned up, and it freaks you out to have somebody looking at you with pure white eyes! So in every culture the eyes are closed immediately after death.

But everybody dies with open eyes. Nobody can die with closed eyes, because closing the lids of the eyes needs a certain willpower, a certain life energy. You cannot die with a fist, because the fist needs some life energy. You can die only with an open hand, because an open hand is relaxed, it needs no life, no energy. In the same way, everybody dies with open eyes. And not to make others freak out, immediately the older people pull the eyelids down. The old fellow who has died cannot now even open them again, because for that too some energy is needed. He may want to have a look—what is happening around?—but he cannot open them.

So it is nothing special about Ma Tzu that he touched his nose with his tongue. The special thing is that people ordinarily don't try it; otherwise everybody can touch. It is just that your teeth are the barrier. So whenever by chance your teeth fall out, and they will fall out one day, then try it and you will find that Ma Tzu was not doing some great miraculous thing, he was just very old.

In India they have the idea that on the feet of a buddha, on the underneath of the feet, there are two rings. They are the signs, when a child is born, that the person will become a buddha. It is not necessary for every buddha to have those two rings, but any child that is born with those two rings is inevitably going to become a buddha.

It is not inevitable for everybody. You may become or you may not become, it is your choice. But it is not a choice for a man like Ma Tzu. He had earned enough from his meditation in his past life, and was so close to buddhahood when he died that it was absolutely certain he would become a buddha.

Perhaps Enō had seen those two rings on his feet when he said to Nangaku, "This young man is going to become a buddha. I am old, and he is asking for initiation, but you are going to be my successor, so it is better that you take care of him from the very beginning. Give him initiation, and remember, be respectful to him. He is already a buddha—just a little push and he will be on the other shore."

The story Maneesha has brought:
Ma Tzu had three outstanding disciples who enjoyed a special intimacy with him. They were Nan-chuan, Chih-tsang, and Hui-hai (otherwise known as Hyakujō).

It is almost inevitable from the way ancient masters worked that there will be a certain intimacy between them and a few disciples. They may have thousands of disciples, but a few disciples will be intimate. From these intimate disciples will be chosen their successor.

It is no more applicable as far as I am concerned because nobody is going to be a successor to me. The very idea of succeeding was an idea borrowed from the royal families. Just as kings were succeeded by their eldest sons, it reflected on the tradition of masters also that somebody would become their successor.

I want to make a complete break. As far as I am concerned, you are all intimate to me. I can afford the intimacy of all of you, because there is no question of any succeeding. Nobody is going to be my successor. I want everybody to be a master unto himself.

To be a successor is a little humiliating. It is against the dignity of an enlightened man. Neither has he anybody before him as his predecessor nor has he anybody after him who is his successor. He is alone, standing like an Everest; no one precedes him, no one succeeds him.

His aloneness is a message to all who fall in love with him, that they also have to be alone. In your aloneness you are beautiful, pure. It does not mean that you have to renounce the world. It simply means that you don't have to belong to the world. You can remain in the marketplace, but just be a mirror, a witness, watching whatever is going on.

But traditionally they never understood that it is against the freedom of the individual to be a successor. It makes a spiritual experience almost like a treasury or a kingdom. It is neither. Nobody can succeed. Everybody has to be on his own, and that independence and the taste of that independence is so valuable that I want to bring a new kind of master and a new kind of disciple into the world. They are intimate in their love, in their trust, but they are not bound in any way—by any thread, visible or invisible. The master is himself, the disciple is also himself. And the function of the master is to prove to the disciple that to be oneself is the greatest glory in the world, the most splendorous thing.

But Ma Tzu is old...part of the old world. He had these three disciples as intimate disciples—Nan-chuan, Chih-tsang, and Hui-hai (otherwise known as Hyakujō). Nan-chuan is better known as Nansen. He had a special place in the master's heart, but in the line of transmission, Hyakujō became the successor of Ma Tzu.

One evening, as the three disciples were attending on their master,

*enjoying the moon together, he asked them what they thought would be
the best way of spending such a night.*

*Chih-tsang was the first to answer. He said, "A good time to make
offerings"*—a good time to feel grateful to existence.

Hui-hai said, "A good time to cultivate one's spiritual life."

Nan-chuan made no answer, but shook his sleeves and went away.

*Ma Tzu turned to Chih-tsang and said, "The sutras will join
the tsang."*

*(He was making a pun on Chih-tsang's name, tsang, which in Chinese
means 'basket', as in carrying the word of Buddha.)*

Buddha's sutras are divided into three baskets. Ma Tzu said to
Chih-tsang, just making a pun on his name, "You will be one of the
enlightened ones who will carry the Buddha's sutras. You will be a
basket to carry the Buddha's sutras. You will be a great scholar." And
that's how it came to be.

A master's insight, his clarity, is always, twenty-four hours a day,
the same. He could see through this man although he is just making
a pun on his name. But he uses even that opportunity to indicate to
him that he will be a great scholar.

He turned to Hui-hai and said: "Dhyana will return to the sea."

*(Ma Tzu was making a second pun, since, in Chinese, hai means
'sea'.)*

Hui-hai had said that it was a good time for cultivating spirituality. And the way to cultivate spirituality is *dhyana*, meditation. His
Chinese name 'hai' means 'sea'. And every meditation is bringing
your small river of life to the great ocean of existence, to the sea.

So Ma Tzu was saying to Hui-hai, "You will reach the sea." And
Hui-hai became a great enlightened master. Then Ma Tzu concluded, "Nan-chuan alone transcends the realm of all things, all by
himself." Nan-chuan had not answered. On the contrary he simply
left the place. His gesture shows that talking about scriptures is not
the right way, talking about cultivating spirituality is absolutely
absurd. You cannot cultivate it, it is already there. Hence he did not
answer. And rather than answering, he shook his sleeves and went
away. This was his answer.

In Zen you have to understand that even a gesture is an answer. It is wordless, but he is answering. He is saying, "Keep your scriptures and keep cultivating your spirituality, I am leaving. This is not my place. I am already a buddha, I have nothing to do. Cultivating spirituality or becoming a great scholar, these are not for me. These are for ordinary human beings."

It is said in histories of Zen that Nan-chuan, known as Nansen, had a special place in the master's heart. He was a very beautiful man with great understanding. He went deeper into meditation and finally became an enlightened master. Everybody was thinking that Nansen would be chosen as the successor. But in the line of transmission, Hyakujō became the successor of Ma Tzu.

It shows something very special, that it does not matter who is closer to your heart; what matters is who is closer to truth. Ma Tzu loved Nansen, and everybody thought that he would be chosen. But finally, before his death, he chose Hyakujō, because he was the man who was closest to the truth. He may not be close to his heart; it does not matter. It is not a personal transmission. It is a universal phenomenon, that the lamp of enlightenment should be transmitted to whomever is closer to the ultimate truth.

On another occasion a monk asked Ma Tzu, "What is the Buddha?"
Ma Tzu answered, "Mind is the Buddha."
Listen very carefully because these are very great statements.
Ma Tzu answered, "Mind is the Buddha."
The monk then asked, "What is the Way?"
"No-mind is the Way," answered Ma Tzu.
Now he is being his strange self. First he says, "*Mind is the Buddha.*" And when asked, "*What is the Way?*" he says, "*No-mind is the Way.*" He is canceling mind and making no-mind the way. Mind becomes no-mind, if it is empty. No-mind is not some other entity. No-mind is the same entity as the mind; the difference is whether the mind is full of thoughts, or empty of thoughts. If empty, it is no-mind, if full of thoughts, it is mind.

So he did well in answering slowly because a sudden answer may not be understood. He said, "*Mind is the Buddha.*" It feels consoling —you have the mind, so Buddha is not far away.

The monk then asked, "What is the Way?"
And then he plays his trick. He says, *"No-mind is the Way"*—you
will have to empty the mind of all its content.
*The monk then asked, "Are the Buddha and the Way somewhat
different?"*
*Ma Tzu replied, "The Buddha is like stretching out the hand, the Way
is like clenching the fist."*
There is no real difference. My hand open, or my hand as a fist—
it is the same thing, just different formations of the same thing. It is a
very beautiful statement, that the Buddha and the way are almost the
same. As you travel the path you become inch by inch, every day, a
buddha. It is just like a sculpture. If you are making a statue of
Gautam Buddha, you cannot make it completely in one stroke. You
will have to take out, chunk by chunk, pieces that are not necessary,
to cut the marble into the shape of Gautam Buddha.

That's exactly what you are doing with yourself. In meditation,
every day, you are dropping something and gaining something deeper
into your being. You are dropping some chunk of the marble and
making clear at least a part of the buddha.

Slowly slowly the whole buddha arises in its totality, and in that
moment you disappear. In that moment only buddha remains in you,
you are the buddha. The path, the traveler and the goal are only
different stages of the same phenomenon.

A poem by Ikkyū:

What a naughty fellow he was,
The man who was called Sakya!
By him many people are driven to puzzling.

Sakya is Gautam Buddha's family name. Ikkyū is saying what a
naughty fellow he was, that many people were driven by him to
puzzling.

It is true. For twenty-five centuries continuously Gautam Buddha
has been harassing people. I am harassing you every night; whether
you want to be a buddha or not, I am intent that you have to become
a buddha.

Ikkyū is saying it out of love, it is not derogatory. He is simply saying, "What a naughty fellow!" Twenty-five centuries after Gautam Buddha, people are still puzzling how to become a buddha. As long as man exists on the earth this is going to remain a puzzling matter, because nobody else in the whole sky of consciousness seems to have puzzled humanity as much as Gautam Buddha. He insisted on originality, he insisted on your authentic being, he wanted your total freedom. No man has loved humanity so much. No man has given more dignity to man than Gautam Buddha. He does not want you to become a follower, he wants you to become a buddha.

All great religious teachers, compared to Gautam Buddha, fall very short. They want you to become followers, they want you to practice a certain discipline, they want you to manage your affairs, your morality, your lifestyle. They make a mold of you and they give you a beautiful prison cell.

Buddha stands alone, totally for freedom. Without freedom man cannot know his ultimate mystery; chained he cannot move his wings into the sky and cannot go into the beyond. Every religion is chaining people, keeping some hold on them, not allowing them to be their original beings, but giving them personalities and masks— and this they call religious education.

Buddha does not give you any religious education. He wants you simply to be yourself, whatever it is. That is your religion—to be yourself. No man has loved freedom so much. No man has loved mankind so much. He would not accept followers for the simple reason that to accept a follower is to destroy his dignity. He accepted only fellow travelers. His last statement before dying was, "If I ever come back, I will come as your friend." Maitreya means the friend.

Maneesha has asked:

Our Beloved Master,
Who of us here would not like to "enjoy a special intimacy" with our master, to have a special place in his heart?
What is it to be truly intimate with You?

Maneesha, my heart is empty. And the more empty you become,

the more you can be intimate with me. You will be intimate with me in becoming an empty heart. Then you will be falling into the same tune, the same dance, the same music. And this intimacy is not the old intimacy we talked about. It is a totally different intimacy, qualitatively different. I may not even know your name, you may have never met me personally, but still you can be intimate with me, because I am giving intimacy a totally new dimension. If your heart is empty, suddenly you will be in tune with me. And this intimacy will not create any jealousy.

All those old intimacies were creating jealousies even in the masters' assemblies. If three persons were intimate, do you think others were not offended? Do you think others were not jealous? Everybody wants to be specially intimate. That was not possible in the old way, but my definition of intimacy is such that the whole universe can be intimate with me without creating any jealousy in anybody.

You can be intimate because it is not dependent on me, it is dependent on you. You empty your heart and in that emptying of the heart you will become my intimate. You may be on another planet, that does not matter. And in this dimension of intimacy, there is no limitation. Everybody can be specially intimate to me.

Now it is time for something serious. Sardar Gurudayal Singh, you are getting old, but you will not leave your ancient habit!

It is Ronald Reagan's birthday, and Nancy wants to make him his favorite spaghetti sauce for dinner. So she goes to Giovanni and asks for some tomatoes.

"Sorry," says Giovanni, "we have-a no tomatoes."

"But you must have tomatoes," insists Nancy. "It is Ronnie's birthday, and I want to make his favorite spaghetti sauce."

"Sorry," repeats Giovanni, "we have-a no tomatoes."

"But that's ridiculous," whines Nancy. "Can't you call your wife, Maria? Maybe she has some tomatoes?"

"Look," insists Giovanni, "we have-a no tomatoes!"

But Nancy keeps on whining.

"Okay!" shouts Giovanni. "Tell-a me something. What do you get-a when you take the 'pine' out of pineapple?"

"Apple," replies Nancy.

"Right!" says Giovanni. "And what do you get-a when you take the 'gr' out of grape?"

"Ape," says Nancy.

"Good!" says Giovanni. "And what do you get-a when you take the 'fuck' out of tomatoes?"

Nancy pauses, and then says, "But there is no 'fuck' in tomatoes."

Giovanni screams, "That is-a what I've been trying to tell you!"

Paddy has been drinking a few whiskeys and needs to go to the bathroom. He gets up from the bar and staggers across the floor past Gorgeous Gloria, who is sitting at one of the tables in her new maxi-mini skirt.

Distracted by her long, lean, bare legs, the drunken Paddy trips over her chair, stumbles, and falls to the floor. Gloria jumps up and stands over him trying to help him to get up.

Paddy cannot help taking a look under her skirt.

"Mister Murphy," exclaims Gloria, crossing her legs, "I thought you were a gentleman!"

"It is okay, Gloria," murmurs Paddy, "I thought you were a blonde!"

Little Ernie comes back from the movies.

"What did you see?" asks his mom.

"Linda Lovelace's 'Deep Throat,'" replies Ernie casually. "It was quite good."

"My God!" cries Ernie's mother. "You saw 'Deep Throat'? But that is an X-rated movie!"

"Well, so what?" says Ernie. "They are all the same. In the G-rated movie, the good guy gets the girl; in the R-rated movie, the bad guy gets the girl; and in the X-rated movie, everybody gets the girl!"

Moishe Finklestein goes into the Ritzy Glitz Restaurant and treats himself to a huge meal with lots of champagne, finishing up with a Havana cigar.

Finally the waiter brings the bill on a silver tray. It comes to ninety-nine dollars and ninety-nine cents, so Moishe pays him with a hundred-dollar bill.

About five minutes later, he calls the waiter back and asks for his change. Without altering his expression, the waiter leaves and returns a moment later with the silver tray. On it is a penny and a packet of condoms.

Moishe is shocked, and demands an explanation. The waiter lifts his nose in the air, and says, "Sir, it is the policy of our restaurant to encourage customers like you not to reproduce!"

Nivedano...

Nivedano...

Be silent.
Close your eyes.
Feel the body to be completely frozen.
Now look inwards with total urgency
as if there is not going to be another moment.
Only with such urgency,
as if this is the last moment of your life,
can your vision penetrate
to your life sources,
to your eternity,
to your buddha.
Deeper and deeper,
because you are not going to be a loser,
you are going to gain your lost kingdom.
You have been living outside in a dream;
inside you at the deepest center
is just a watcher,
unclouded, unattached, unidentified,
the mirror of your very being
which simply reflects.
This mirror has been called the buddha.
And you all have it.
It is nothing personal,
it is universal.

To make it more clear, Nivedano...

Relax.

Just let your body be there
and your mind,
but remember that you are only a watcher.
You are neither the body nor the mind,
but only a mirror reflecting,
without any judgment,
a pure reflection of the moon in the lake.
This is your ultimate reality.
This is your very being.
It is beyond words, but not beyond experience.
It is your very sky, without any limitations.
This fortunate evening,
ten thousand buddhas have disappeared
into an oceanic awareness,
just pure consciousness.
The Buddha Auditorium has become just a lake
of reflecting consciousnesses.
Rejoice in it.
Let it go deep
into every fiber of your being,
so that slowly, slowly your every action is filled
with your self-nature;
so that twenty-four hours you are a buddha.
The day you don't need to meditate
is the greatest day of your life.
A buddha does not meditate,
he *is* meditation.
Gather the experience, remember the way—
no-mind is the way—
and remember the blessings, the ecstasy
that is now in this moment
showering on you.
All these flowers, all these roses,
bring their perfume at least with you.

Nivedano...

Come back,
but come back as a buddha,
carrying the buddha gracefully.
Sit down just like the buddha.
This moment you have made this place holy,
this evening immortal,
this moment your very eternity.
Satyam, Shivam, Sundram.
The truth, the good and the beautiful.
This is your original face.

Okay, Maneesha?
Yes, Beloved Master.
Can we celebrate the gathering of ten thousand
buddhas?
Yes, Beloved Master.

the hunter

Our Beloved Master,

Ma Tzu was noted for his resourcefulness in finding expedient means of working with his disciples. This is illustrated by his conversion of Shih-kung, who was originally a hunter, loathing the very sight of Buddhist monks. One day, as he was chasing after a deer, he passed by Ma Tzu's monastery. Ma Tzu came forward to meet him. Shih-kung asked him whether he had seen any deer pass by.

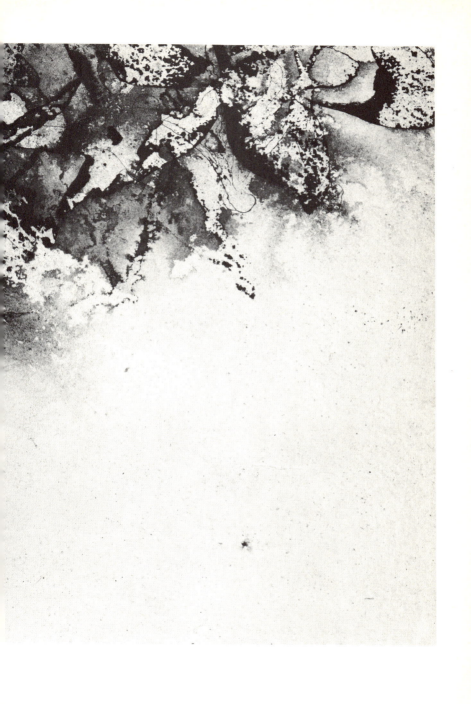

Ma Tzu asked, "Who are you?"

"A hunter," he replied.

"Do you know how to shoot?" queried Ma Tzu.

"Of course I do," replied the hunter.

"How many can you hit with one arrow?" asked Ma Tzu.

"One arrow can only shoot down one deer," said Shih-kung.

"In that case, you really don't know how to shoot," Ma Tzu commented.

The hunter then asked Ma Tzu, "Does your reverence know how to shoot?"

Ma Tzu replied, "Of course I do."

"How many can you kill with one arrow?" the hunter asked.

"I can kill a whole flock with a single arrow," answered the master.

At this, Shih-kung said, "The beasts have life as you do: why should you shoot down a whole flock?"

Ma Tzu said, "Since you know this so well, why don't you shoot yourself?"

Shih-kung answered, "Even if I wanted to shoot myself, I would not know how to manage it."

At this point, Ma Tzu remarked, "This fellow has accumulated klesa from ignorance for numberless aeons. Today the whole process has come to a sudden stop."

Tossing his arrows and bows to the ground, Shih-kung became a monk and a disciple of Ma Tzu.

Some time later, when Shih-kung was working in the kitchen, Ma Tzu asked him what he was doing.

"I am tending an ox," the disciple answered.

"How do you tend it?" asked Ma Tzu.

Shih-kung replied, "As soon as it returns to the grass, I ruthlessly pull it back by its nostrils."

This won great approval from the master, who remarked, "You certainly know the true way of tending an ox!"

maneesha, there are two kinds of masters, not in any way different in their experiences, but different in conveying their experience to others.

One is simply using old methods, well tried, which have given sure results. The other is a creative person, who does not follow any traditional method or device to transform a person, but responds to each person according to his need.

Ma Tzu belongs to the second category, of very creative and inventive masters. He never repeats himself. In every situation he will bring a new device; he will function just as a mirror. And whatever comes spontaneously out of his empty heart, he will use it as a vehicle of *dhamma*.

This type of master is very rare, because you don't know whether a method is going to succeed; you don't know what will be the outcome. You are simply trusting in your own heart, that your heart cannot let you down. This is an immense trust in one's own enlightenment and awakening—that whatever comes out of your illumination is going to succeed, there is no question about it. Hence a man like Ma Tzu has a tremendous freedom.

Other masters have thousands of methods given by the tradition, and they choose one of them; but it is a dead device, even though success seems to be more certain.

With Ma Tzu success is not the point; success is the last point in the journey. All those masters in the first category are looking at the success—the method *must* succeed. And because the method has been used again and again, and has been successful, why bother to look for a new method? Their emphasis is on the end, the success.

Ma Tzu's method, his approach, is totally different. It depends on the first point of the journey, from where the arrow comes. If it is coming from your empty heart, then there is no need to bother about success. That is no more the question for Ma Tzu. His whole life he invented thousands of methods, according to the person confronting him. And he had tremendous success.

But his success is the success of the empty mirror. He reflects the man so accurately that there is no need to fall back on old methods. He can go straight forward with the man who is confronting him, and make a situation in which the transmission happens; in which, heart to heart, something moves, something is inspired, something takes the light from one heart to the other heart.

It is said about him:

*With Ma Tzu, Zen took on a truly Chinese flavor—open-hearted and
not highly controlled. Under Ma Tzu, mysterious meditation and
renunciation for the practice of Zazen in the mountains dropped.
The speciality of Zen after Ma Tzu was nothing but the fragrance of
intense living.*

He reduced everything to intense inquiry, intense living. Intensity
became the focus of his whole teaching.

One hundred and thirty persons became enlightened under Ma
Tzu. Just as an example of his working...

*Ma Tzu was noted for his resourcefulness in finding expedient means
of working with his disciples. This is illustrated by his conversion of
Shih-kung, who was originally a hunter, loathing the very sight of
Buddhist monks. One day, as he was chasing after a deer, he passed by
Ma Tzu's monastery. Ma Tzu came forward to meet him. Shih-kung
asked him whether he had seen any deer pass by.*

Ma Tzu asked, "Who are you?"

Now, it is out of the blue...Shih-kung is asking about the deer,
and Ma Tzu changes the whole situation into a totally new dimension. Such was his resourcefulness.

Ma Tzu asked, "Who are you?"

This was not an answer, certainly, to the question asked.

"A hunter," he replied.

"Do you know how to shoot?"

He has changed the whole subject matter.

"Do you know how to shoot?" queried Ma Tzu.

"Of course I do," replied the hunter.

"How many can you hit with one arrow?" asked Ma Tzu.

"One arrow can only shoot down one deer," said Shih-kung.

"In that case, you really don't know how to shoot."

Do you see the shifting of the situation? Slowly he is bringing him
to a totally different thing. Shih-kung has simply asked, "Have you
seen any deer pass?" He has not come for renunciation, he has not
come for initiation, he is not there for any inquiry into truth. But it
does not matter—once you have come in front of Ma Tzu, you will
not be able to leave that place unchanged. Just the very touch of Ma
Tzu's air is enough to make a difference.

He said to Shih-kung: *"In that case you really don't know how to shoot."*

The hunter then asked Ma Tzu, "Does your reverence know how to shoot?"

Ma Tzu replied, "Of course I do."

"How many can you kill with one arrow?" the hunter asked.

"I can kill a whole flock with a single arrow," answered the master. At this, Shih-kung said...

Now you see the climate changing—he has forgotten about the deer and the hunting.

At this, Shih-kung said, "The beasts have life as you do..." Killing the whole flock, it is so life-negative—and for a master like you...*"why should you shoot down a whole flock?"*

Ma Tzu said, "Since you know this so well, why don't you shoot yourself?"

Searching for deer to shoot...the deer has life, you have life—why go just so far, why not shoot yourself? You are intelligent enough to understand that the whole flock should not be shot. But if you understand that much—that the whole flock should not be shot— why should one deer be shot? The principle is the same: don't destroy life. And if you are intent on destroying life...

"Since you know this so well," said Ma Tzu, *"why don't you shoot yourself?"*

What does it matter whose life is lost—whether it is a deer's life or your life?

Shih-kung answered, *"Even if I wanted to shoot myself, I would not know how to manage it."*

Shooting oneself is almost impossible with an arrow. With a gun, that is a different matter: you can just put it to the side of your head, and you are gone! But for an arrow, space is needed; you cannot manage to shoot yourself with an arrow, it is almost an impossibility.

At this point, Ma Tzu remarked, *"This fellow has accumulated* klesa *from ignorance for numberless aeons."*

Klesa is a Sanskrit word; it means, originally, evil, misery, suffering, torturing others and oneself.

Ma Tzu said, *"This fellow has accumulated* klesa *from ignorance for numberless aeons. Today the whole process has come to a sudden stop."*

He cannot shoot himself, and he has been shooting for his whole life—perhaps for many lives.

Tossing his arrows and bows to the ground, Shih-kung became a monk and a disciple of Ma Tzu.

Do you see that no device has been used? It is not a device at all; just a simple conversation in which he turns the whole subject matter to a point where the hunter becomes aware that to kill life is ugly.

Up to now he was boasting that he is a great hunter. To destroy his ego of being a hunter, Ma Tzu is saying to him, "The best way to prove that you are a hunter is: shoot yourself!"

The poor hunter came to a full stop, because you cannot shoot yourself with an arrow. In that silence, in which he started thinking how to shoot himself, he forgot all about deer, he forgot that he was a hunter. In that small gap of silence, Ma Tzu entered into his heart. This is not visible in the story, it cannot be visible in words.

In that full stop, his mind could not function anymore; and the non-functioning of the mind is the right time for a master to enter into the very heart of the disciple. It does not need any effort on the part of the master—it simply and spontaneously happens. Once the gap is there, the same light, the same awakening, enters into the man confronting the master.

The hunter did not answer. He threw his bow and his arrows on the ground, and fell to the feet of Ma Tzu, and asked for initiation. He had come for a different purpose, and got caught in the net of Ma Tzu.

It was not even a device, but this is how Ma Tzu was resourceful. He would convert any situation in such a subtle way that the person would not be even aware that he was being brought to a new space.

Shih-kung saw the whole situation: that he had been destroying life, and to destroy life is absolutely wrong. He dropped his bow, his arrows...a sudden awakening, that it is time to search, not for the deer, but for himself, for the source of life itself. He became a disciple of Ma Tzu. He started working in Ma Tzu's temple.

Ma Tzu asked him one day what he was doing.

"I am tending an ox," the disciple answered.

I have to explain to you that "I am tending an ox" does not mean exactly what it says. It is a symbolic saying in Zen.

There are ten cards in Tao, just like tarot cards. Those cards are called "tending an ox." The ox is a symbol of your own self. Searching for the self is the meaning of those symbolic cards.

When those cards were brought from China to Japan, the last card was dropped for specific reasons: it needed tremendously great understanding for the tenth card. Those cards had been made according to Buddha's own description.

In the first card the ox has escaped into the forest. A man, the owner, is standing, looking all around, and there is no sign of the ox.

In the second card, he finds the footprints on the earth. He follows the footprints.

In the third card, he sees the ox's back, his tail. He is hiding behind a big tree.

In the fourth card, he sees the whole ox.

In the fifth, he catches hold of him.

In the sixth, he is fighting hard to take him back to the house.

In the seventh, he is victorious.

In the eighth, he is riding on the ox, coming back towards home.

In the ninth, the ox is in its stall, and the man is playing a song on his flute.

These nine cards were taken out of a pack of ten cards. In China originally, and in Buddha's statement also, a tenth card is described. But it really needs guts to understand the tenth card. Even the Japanese masters thought it is better to drop it, because it is very difficult to make people understand it. Even Buddha said, "I am at the ninth card"—because the tenth is certainly difficult.

The tenth shows that the man, feeling so happy that he has found his ox, takes up a whiskey bottle and goes towards the pub.

Now that is very difficult—a buddha with a whiskey bottle going towards the pub!

But I don't want to drop the tenth card, because it is as symbolic as the other cards. You accept the ox as yourself; you accept the search and inquiry as your meditation. Part by part you become aware of your inner reality.

The tenth is the ultimate point, when you become intoxicated with the universe. That whiskey bottle is not a whiskey bottle—just as the ox is not the ox—they are all symbols.

Those masters who dropped that card were a little weaker. It was so simple to explain it: that when you have found yourself, you have found the ultimate nectar; you will be drunk twenty-four hours a day. You don't need ordinary alcohol, you don't need any drug—your very experience will be a drug.

And you all know after your meditation, when you start moving towards the canteen—I have been watching—everybody looks drunk. A few get up early, but very reluctantly; a few are sitting still, utterly drunk, remembering finally that they have to go to the canteen. This drunkenness...

By the way, I want to tell you that it is the only possibility for humanity to get rid of all drugs, of all alcohol, because they are very ordinary compared to the purity of the drunkenness that happens at the very source of life. Nothing is comparable to it. It takes you higher, it gives you tremendous euphoria—which is not hallucination—and it lasts. It is not a question of taking the drug in greater and greater quantities, of becoming addicted to it. You become the nectar itself, you become the euphoria, the ecstasy itself. You don't need anything; just remembering your buddhahood is enough to live with immense ecstasy in your day-to-day life.

So this "tending an ox," you should remember, is an old metaphor for searching for the self. Otherwise you will not be able to understand the anecdote.

The disciple answered, *"I am tending an ox."*

"How do you tend it?" asked Ma Tzu.

Shih-kung replied, "As soon as it returns to the grass, I ruthlessly pull it back by its nostrils."

This won great approval from the master, who remarked,

"You certainly know the true way of tending an ox!"

As an anecdote in itself, if you don't know its connotations, it is absurd. But if you understand it with all the metaphors...because these anecdotes carry a tremendous tradition.

Shih-kung replied, "As soon as it returns to the grass..." Do you understand? We use the word 'grass' for the mundane also; for the rude, for the primitive, for the uncivilized, uncultured.

Shih-kung says, "As soon *as it returns to the grass*—to the mundane *—I ruthlessly pull it back by its nostrils.*" He is saying that he does not allow himself to be attracted by the grass. He pulls himself away from the grass, towards the great, towards the magnificent, towards the inner splendor.

If you understand this connotation, then you will be able to understand why the master approved it.

This won great approval from the master, who remarked, "You certainly know the true way of tending an ox!"

Soseki wrote:

When the master without a word
raises his eyebrows,
the posts and rafters,
the crossbeams and roof tree,
begin to smile.
There is another place for
conversing heart to heart:
the full moon and the breeze
at the half-open window.

Soseki is a well known mystic poet and master. What he is saying cannot be said in prose.

When the master without a word
raises his eyebrows,
the posts and rafters,
the crossbeams and roof tree,
begin to smile.
There is another place for
conversing heart to heart:
the full moon and the breeze
at the half-open window.

Just standing at the half-open window, the cool breeze and the full moon, and utter silence in between...

A master is a door to the universe; a master in himself is an empty heart. You can see the whole universe through it. Coming closer to the master in deep love and trust, even his raising of his eyebrows triggers something in you.

...The posts and rafters, the crossbeams and roof tree, begin to smile.

Even the posts and the rafters, in the presence of a master, start to smile. The whole existence smiles in the presence of a master, for the simple reason that at least part of us has reached to the ultimate expression of our potentiality. And he is a symbol that we can also reach to the same height, to the same depth.

The disciple's heart immensely rejoices in the master's presence—just his presence. He may not say a single word, he may remain silent, but just his presence takes you to another world of silence and peace, of love and joy, of blessings that you have not even dreamed of.

Maneesha has asked a question:

Our Beloved Master,
There could never have been a master more resourceful in finding expedient means of working with his disciples than You.
Who else would create a concoction of zany anecdotes, serious sutras, wild dancing, automated animals, jokes, gibberish and silence such as You serve up each evening?
In the context of You, somehow everything feels so absolutely right.

Maneesha, it *is* absolutely right, it is just that in my context you become aware of it. It is as if all the lights go out: these ten thousand buddhas will be still sitting here, but you will not be able to see them. Then the lights come on, and suddenly you see ten thousand people sitting around you. You were not alone in the darkness.

The context of the master is simply a light in your darkness. Everything seems to be true, everything seems to be beautiful—but it is not the master's light that is making them beautiful. They are beautiful in themselves, but a light is needed to see them.

If you grow your own light, the master's context will not be needed.

The master's whole effort is that he should not be needed; that you should be enough unto yourself; that your own light should shine and radiate; that the existence should smile with your smiling heart.

It is true that I am a little crazy. (*Sardarji's familiar laugh comes loudly from the back of the auditorium.*) Now, Sardarji, I have not yet told the joke, don't trust me too much!

I use everything, that's why I said that the Japanese masters who brought those ten cards and dropped one on the way were not very courageous. They were intelligent, but not geniuses. They could not find an explanation for the tenth card.

And to me, without the tenth card the nine are useless. What is the point of searching for yourself? The whole point is to become a drunk! The tenth card is the most essential, but even Gautam Buddha was afraid. Although he described the ten cards, he said, "I am myself at the ninth," just to avoid the complication of the tenth. The bottle of alcohol in the hands of a buddha simply does not look right. Even he avoided the tenth card—but I will not avoid it.

In many countries, sannyasins wanted to take my picture with a bottle, to make the tenth card. I said, "It is perfectly okay, just fill the bottle with Coca-Cola! It is so simple, because in the photograph it won't show that there is Coca-Cola, and your purpose will be served."

I am just a little crazy, not too much.

You are right, that nobody has worked the way I work. And I love to work in every possible way—not denying anything—a total approval of life and all its turns, all its paths. I have accepted it in its totality, so I can use anything as an indicator. And from any point of view I can bring you to seek and search for the escaped ox.

Now, Sardarji's time has come at last!

Before you go into your meditations, in search of the ox, it is perfectly good to go in a happy mood; not serious, but smiling. Remember it: existence smiles when you smile, and when you are serious you are alone. Existence does not bother about your seriousness. If you want the whole world with you, just smile, and look all around and you will see trees smiling, and the flowers smiling. And at least when you are entering into meditation, it is good to enter with a smiling heart.

I have used jokes for the first time in the whole history of mankind, because such beautiful jokes...and nobody has used them for meditation. And they create such a good feeling all around, that one becomes courageous enough. A laughing heart is more courageous than a serious one. A serious heart doubts, hesitates, thinks twice. The laughing one is the heart of the gambler, he simply jumps in. And meditation is a question of jumping into the unknown.

Friar Fruck, the Jesuit missionary, is in Africa looking for a few Christian converts. He is marching across the plains with his crucifix and Holy Bible in hand, when suddenly he comes face to face with a huge, ferocious lion.

Friar Fruck's eyes roll to the back of his head, and he drops to his knees in a near-faint.

"Beloved God Almighty, King of Kings, all-knowing, all-seeing Father of the world," pleads Friar Fruck, praying feverishly, "save my blessed ass!"

The lion watches the Christian closely, and then he bows his own head, crosses his paws, and murmurs in a soft growl, "Beloved God Almighty, King of beasts and Lord of the jungle, please bless this poor food I am about to eat!"

Angela Angelovitch, the greatest ballet dancer in living memory, is going to give her last performance.

"Angela," says Petrov, her manager, "for this performance, you must give everything, *everything!*"

That night, when the curtains are drawn back, Angela is standing on a platform, high above the stage, wearing a small pair of wings. The orchestra is playing and Angela leaps into the air and lands gracefully on the stage, to loud cheers.

Immediately, Angela jumps up and daintily climbs a ladder, and goes even higher than before. The orchestra plays loudly, and Angela springs into space. She spins through the air and lands on her tiptoes.

A rope descends and, to thundering applause, Angela is lifted right to the roof. The drums roll and then there is a deathly hush.

Angela jumps. She flies, spinning through the air, and lands in the middle of the stage with her legs apart, in a perfect split. The audience is hysterical.

At last, the curtains close and the audience starts to go home. Angela is resting motionless on the stage. Her legs are still split wide apart.

"Bravo! Encore!" shouts Petrov, her manager, walking onto the stage, clapping his hands.

"Petrov," says Angela, "will you do me a favor?"

"Yes, my darling," replies Petrov, "after a performance like that, anything!"

"Okay," says Angela, "then rock me a little, and break the suction!"

Just take your time! Has everybody got it?

Where is Haridas?—because he is the polar opposite of Sardarji. They both are great friends, and their friendship depends on one thing: Sardarji can get any kind of joke, Haridas never gets any! So he laughs—what else to do? Understanding is not his thing.

Swami Deva Coconut is standing in his bamboo house watching the waters rise around his ankles. It has been raining constantly for four days and the sky is still grey and wet.

As the water reaches his knees, Coconut climbs onto his suitcase, and when the water reaches to his knees again, he goes outside and climbs onto the roof of his bamboo house.

Just then, Ma Mango Milkshake comes past on a small raft.

"Come on, Coconut!" she calls out, "come for a ride!"

"No thanks," he replies. "I am just going to wait here, and watch."

Slowly, the water climbs up the side of the bamboo house, and starts to wash against Coconut's ankles again.

Swami Cleverhead, the group leader, rows up in a small rowboat. The boat is leaking water fast, but Cleverhead seems to be managing.

"Come on, Coconut!" calls Cleverhead. "Let us go out of here!"

"No thanks," replies Coconut. "I'm just waiting here and watching."

A half an hour later, Coconut has water around his neck, on top of his bamboo house.

Just then, Captain Cliffski and Captain Kurtski, the famous Polack pilots, fly over in a borrowed helicopter.

Captain Cliffski sees Coconut, and leans out of the window.

"Come on now, Coconut!" he shouts, "or you are going to be drowned!"

Coconut waves back, "I am just waiting here and watching!" he shouts.

Later, somewhere in the realms of the universe, Swami Deva Coconut meets Osho Rajneesh, and he seems really pissed off about something.

"I waited and I waited, I watched, I witnessed," exclaims Coconut, "and you never came to rescue me!"

"My God!" says Osho Rajneesh, "I sent you two boats and a helicopter!"

Big Rock Hunk, the famous Hollywood movie star, walks into the lobby of the exclusive Screwing Sands Hotel, and accidentally hits Gorgeous Gloria on the chest with his elbow.

"I'm extremely sorry," says Rock, sweetly, "but if your heart is as soft as your breast, then I am sure you will forgive me."

"That's all right," replies Gloria, "and if the rest of you is as hard as your elbow, my room is number thirty-three!"

Nivedano...

Nivedano…

Be silent. Close your eyes.
Feel your body to be completely frozen.
Look inwards with absolute urgency.
This moment may be the last moment.
Always remember that every moment
is possibly the last moment.
Then your urgency remains total.
Go deeper, as deep as you can,
because it is your own space,
your very life source—nothing to fear.
At the very center of your being you are
connected with the heart of the universe.
Your empty heart becomes a door
to the ultimate heart of the universe.
And the moment you feel you are connected
and rooted in the ultimate,
everything in existence becomes beautiful, blissful.
Not only life, but death also

becomes a dance, a celebration.
Just watch, witness.
Nivedano…

Relax. Let the body lie down.
Remember you are not the body,
nor the mind.
You are the witness, which is far away—
even skies are underneath it.
It is a watcher on the hills.
Your body is in the dark valleys down below.
The distance between your witness
and your body-mind structure is qualitative.
It cannot be bridged.
And people go on living in ignorance,
because they go on thinking
that they are the body, they are the mind.
And because of this identification
with body and mind,
they have forgotten the language of their inner being,
their inner nature, their universality,
their eternity—the buddha.
This beautiful evening.
This dance of the rain
around the Buddha Auditorium,
and ten thousand buddhas in utter silence,
relaxed, centered…
it becomes a miracle.
It is a magic moment.

I can see there are no individuals,
but only an ocean of consciousness.
This is the point
where one becomes ultimately drunk,
drunk without any drugs.
Let this drunkenness sink in every fiber of your being.
Soon you will be coming back.
Fill all your buckets
with the nectar of the living stream of life,
and bring it with you.
Nivedano…

Now, come back as a buddha.
Silently, peacefully, with grace.
Remember how buddha will sit down,
and this remembrance has to become
the very milieu
twenty-four hours around you.
Whatever you do, remember
that the act has to show your self-nature,
your original face, your buddhahood.
Every gesture, every word, every silence
should arise from your spontaneity.
This is authentic religion.

Okay, Maneesha?
Yes, Beloved Master.
Can we celebrate the ten thousand buddhas?
Yes, Beloved Master.

Our Beloved Master,

Yakusan began his Buddhist studies in the school of Vinaya so he was well-versed in scriptural studies and ascetics by the time he was introduced to Zen. He began to feel that these things were not yet the ultimate goal of the spiritual life. He longed for true freedom and purity beyond the formulas of the dharma. So, seeking guidance, he called on Sekitō.

Yakusan said to the master, "I have only a rough knowledge of the three

to the source

vehicles, and the twelve branches of the scriptural teaching. But I hear that in the south there is a teaching about 'pointing directly at the mind of man and attaining buddhahood through the perception of the self-nature.' Now, this is beyond my comprehension. I humbly beseech you to graciously enlighten me on this."

Sekitō replied, "It is to be found neither in affirmation nor in negation, nor in affirming and negating at the same time. So what can you do?"

Yakusan was altogether mystified by these words.

Hence, Sekitō told him frankly, "The cause and occasion of your enlightenment are not present here in this place. You should rather go to visit the great master, Ma Tzu."

Following the suggestion, Yakusan went to pay his respects to Ma Tzu, presenting before him the same request as he had addressed to Sekitō.

Ma Tzu replied, "I sometimes make him raise his eyebrows and turn his eyes; at other times I do not let him raise his eyebrows and turn his eyes. Sometimes it is really he who is raising his eyebrows and turning his eyes; at other times it is really not he who is raising his eyebrows and turning his eyes. How do you understand this?"

At this, Yakusan saw completely eye-to-eye with Ma Tzu and was enlightened. He bowed reverently to the master, who asked him, "What truth do you perceive that you should perform these ceremonies?"

Yakusan said, "When I was with Sekitō, I was like a mosquito crawling on a bronze ox."

Ma Tzu, discerning that the enlightenment was genuine, asked him to take good care of the insight. He attended upon Ma Tzu for three years. One day, Ma Tzu asked again, "What do you see recently?"

Yakusan replied, "The skin has entirely moulted off; there remains only the one, true reality."

Ma Tzu said, "What you have attained is perfectly in tune with the innermost core of your mind, and from thence it has spread into your four limbs. This being the case, it is time to gird your waist with three bamboo splints, and go forth to make your abode on any mountain you may like."

Yakusan replied, "Who am I to set up any abode on any mountain?"

Ma Tzu said, "Not so! One cannot always be traveling without abiding, nor always be abiding without traveling. To advance from where you can no longer advance, and to do what can no longer be done, you must make yourself into a raft or ferryboat for others. It is not for you to abide here forever."

aneesha, it is absolutely necessary to say a few words before I discuss the sutras you have brought to me.

The authentic master is not concerned with gathering a following, more followers, and becoming a great master because of his following. The authentic master is interested in the disciple and his potentiality. And if he sees that this is not the right place for him to flower, the right climate, then he will send him to another master. That used to be in the past a very common phenomenon. There was no rivalry between masters because they were all working for the same truth, for the same ultimate experience.

But the pseudo masters are different and they have taken over the world. The pseudo master forces the disciple to surrender to him. He makes it almost a commitment and if the disciple leaves him, he will feel guilty for it, it will be called betrayal. And the pseudo master never sends his disciples to another master because he sees that this climate, this atmosphere is not perfectly suitable for his growth.

I want you to see the distinction clearly. The pseudo master is interested in satisfying his own ego, how many disciples he has. He is not really concerned with the welfare of the disciple or his growth. His concern is political.

Hindus are worried that the constitution of India allows Mohammedans to marry four women. Now Hindus are worried that sooner or later the Mohammedans will increase in population. The Hindu has only one wife. Even if he produces a child every year, he cannot compete with the Mohammedan. The problem is of the population, because the politics—who is going to be in power—will depend on the population.

What authority has the Vatican pope about truth? What experience, what enlightenment? But still he has six hundred million Catholics around the world. Naturally he is the biggest religious leader. His greatness is not in his experience, his greatness is in the number of followers. And throughout the centuries all the religions have been killing others and converting others to their religion. "Either you come into my religion, or you cannot live." That has been the attitude of the Mohammedans, that has been the attitude of the Christians. Nobody seems to be interested in the individual. They are all on power trips.

Zen gives you a totally different climate. Sometimes masters have even sent their followers to other masters who are against them. It is a very strange phenomenon to the modern eyes, sending someone to your own opponent. But we have to look deep down: if the person can grow more easily in the climate that the opponent master has created, then there is no hesitation in sending him to the other master.

It was a constant transfer of disciples from one master to another. And sometimes it used to be that a master would seem to the disciple too hard and the opponent master would look more soft. The disciple himself would escape to the other master's monastery.

One case I remember… A disciple escaped from his master's monastery because the master was continuously beating, slapping. And he had heard about another master just a few miles away in the mountains who was very soft and very loving, very nice to be with. So he escaped. When he reached to the other master, the other master asked, "Why have you left your own master?"

He told the reason, "He is too hard. He beats, he slaps. And I have heard you are so nice and so loving. That's why I have come here."

The master immediately slapped him and told him, "You idiot, you don't understand the compassion of your master. Just go back! Are you in search of a nice companionship? Are you interested only, urgently, in searching for the truth? Your master is a great man. We don't agree in our principles, that is something aside. As far as his compassion and love are concerned, he is far greater than me. I can only be nice to you.

"You are blind. You could not see when he hits you, with what love, with what care…how much he cares about you! Even though he is getting old, and in hitting you he hurts himself more than he hurts you, but his whole effort is to bring an urgency. He is not going to live long. As a man he is far greater than I am. As a compassionate teacher there is no parallel to him. You just go back. He is the right person as far as you are concerned."

The disciple could not understand. He had heard that this man is against his master, and he says, "I am in disagreement with your master on many points—but that does not mean that your master's compassion is less, that your master's enlightenment is not authentic. I am not so compassionate. I don't hit you because I don't see the urgency. Perhaps in another life you may become enlightened. My care about you is less than his care. He wants you to become enlightened in this life, this moment. I am a little careless, I don't care, and you think it is nice. It is not nice, it is simply my carelessness—whether you become enlightened or not is not my problem. You can enjoy your life and there is eternity available. Sometime, somewhere, you may become enlightened. Why should I bother?"

He came back to his master, touched his feet, and said what had happened. The master said, "Although we are traditionally opponents —our schools are different, our principles, which are nonessential, are different—I have always understood it, that that man is great, greater than people think. His sending you back here is a sign of his greatness. He has shown love towards you by slapping you. He does not slap ordinarily, but he knows perfectly well that a disciple who has been with me for years will not understand anything else than a good slap. Now go into your hut and start meditating on the sound of one hand clapping."

The disciple had been meditating on this koan for three years. Every day he was getting slaps, beatings, because he would think about it all the time, day and night, sitting. He would hear something in the night—the crickets...all is silent, only crickets—and he would get the idea that perhaps this is the sound. He would run to the master, knock on his door, and even before he had said anything the master would slap him and the disciple would say, "At least let me tell you...!"

The master said, "The moment you open your mouth, you are going to say something wrong. So don't unnecessarily waste my time. When you have got it, I will know without your saying it."

A few days passed and the disciple did not come back to report. He used to come every day—sometimes the wind blowing through the pine trees, sometimes the sound of the running water, anything ...and he would immediately think, "Perhaps this is the sound that will satisfy the master as the answer to the question."

But seeing the situation, that he hits you without even listening to your answer... One day the master closed his door as he saw him coming. What kind of master...? He just looked at him and closed the door and said to him through the closed doors, "Go back to your hut and meditate. I am getting old and I cannot hit you every day unnecessarily. I have looked at your face, it is not the sound that you think. Just go."

But for a few days he did not turn up. The master inquired, "What has happened?" People said, "He is just meditating and he is so silent and so peaceful, he looks like a buddha."

The master went there, touched his feet, shook him and told him, "You have heard it. Now it is enough. Come back to the monastery, it is lunch time."

The disciple could not believe that the master touched his feet. And the master said, "You have got it. And you have been sitting hungry for so many days and I was concerned because I was waiting every day for you to come. I enjoy slapping you so much that without you...I was wondering continuously what happened to the great disciple? But I am satisfied. You have got it. Now it is lunch time. Come, follow me."

It was a different climate altogether when there was no rivalry between masters because the aim was the same. Their methods may be different, their devices may be different, but one thing was absolutely certain, they all agreed on one point: that the search for truth is the first priority, and every disciple has to be sent to the right place, to the right master. It does not mean that the master who is sending the disciple is not right; it simply means that his devices will not suit this kind of man. It does not matter even if he has to be sent to the opponent.

These words I am saying with a deep concern because that whole climate of urgency for truth has disappeared from the world. Now there are thousands of pseudo teachers whose whole effort is how to gather followers. All the religions are doing the same. Have you ever heard of a Hindu *shankaracharya* telling to his disciple, "You go to a Mohammedan Sufi mystic," or vice versa? Have you ever heard of any Christian pope sending somebody to a Zen master to learn meditation?

These organized religions are political. Zen is a non-political religiousness. You cannot call it even religion. It is so individualistic and so emphatically concerned only with the potential of the individual. It does not want anything from the individual, it simply wants him to be himself.

At the time of Ma Tzu, there was another great Zen master in China; his name was Sekitō. You are perfectly well acquainted with Sekitō; he is reborn here. Sekitō means stonehead, and this time he is born as Swami Niskriya; I call him Sekitō, stonehead. And I had to send him back to Germany, just for a few weeks, because only stoneheads can hit against other stoneheads in Germany, you cannot send anybody else. So he goes, and hits his head against other heads for a few days. When he gets tired of enlightening other people, he comes back to rest. Right now he is in Germany.

Sekitō was given the name by his master just because he was really a stonehead. Nothing penetrated into his head. You can do everything, nothing makes any difference, because who is hearing? His master used to beat him and he would laugh and he would say, "Do it as much as you can. Just as you are determined to make me enlightened, I am determined not to become enlightened. It is a question of dignity."

Because of this stubbornness—but with so much love, there was no hatred, there was no anger, it was just to show the master—he would say, "If you are stubborn, then don't think that you alone in the world are stubborn; I am also stubborn. Hit me as much as you can. I am not going to become enlightened." That's why he was given the name Sekitō. But poor Sekitō finally had to become enlightened. You cannot escape a master once you are caught in his net.

Ma Tzu and Sekitō were such great masters that it was said that they divided the whole world between them. Their methods and their ways and their workings were absolutely different. They were completely free of any sense of rivalry. Even in such a situation where only two enlightened beings were there and the whole world was available, there was no rivalry. In fact they are reported to have cooperated with each other in bringing others to enlightenment. A case in point is Yakusan. That whole atmosphere, that golden age of search for truth is now just a memory, an echo in the mountains. But it had a beauty which has to be brought back.

Men's whole being should be concerned primarily in searching for his own life sources. But the modern situation is just the opposite. The Hindus have divided the world in a very beautiful way. They have divided the world into four ages. The first age they call the age of truth; the only concern of the people is truth, hence the name of the age is *satyuga*, the age of truth.

The second they call *treta*, a tripod. The first had four legs, it was a table. One leg is lost, now it is a tripod. There is still the search for truth, but the urgency is less, the intensity is less, the balance is less. On four legs the balance is complete; on three legs the balance cannot be complete, but there is still the same search.

The third age they call *dwapar*, two-legged. Now even the balance of *treta*, the second age, is lost. On two legs you cannot make a table, it will be unbalanced, but still half of the urgency is there.

The last age, in which we are living according to Hindu calculations, is called *kaliyuga*; the age of darkness, the age of blindness, the age of no inquiry into truth. People are concerned with mundane things. They devote their whole life to things which prove finally to be junk.

Their whole life could have been a great experiment in enlightenment, in searching for the roots of life, in being utterly fulfilled and contented. They could have gathered all the joy that the universe makes available to you. They could have danced, they could have sung, they could have rejoiced in all the beauties the universe is filled with. But because of their blindness they remained playing with toys; they never bothered that there is anything more than the toys.

In a way this metaphoric division of time has a certain truth in it.

Today it is very difficult to find people—I have found you, working for thirty-five years continuously—it is very difficult to find people who are really ready to take the jump into the universe at any cost. And only those are the fortunate few.

Maneesha has brought a sutra:

Yakusan began his Buddhist studies in the school of Vinaya.

Vinaya is a Buddhist scripture. Its whole name is *Vinaya Pitak*. Buddha spoke for forty-two years continuously, morning and evening, so naturally a tremendous volume of literature has been collected by the disciples. He never wrote anything, these are all notes from the disciples. 'Vinaya' means humbleness, absolute egolessness.

So the disciples who have collected *Vinaya Pitak*, the scripture, they have found Gautam Buddha's teaching to be utterly humble, egoless, at ease with the universe, without any tension. It is one of the most beautiful books in existence. All the sutras lead to silence and peace and compassion.

Yakusan began his Buddhist studies in the school of Vinaya, *so he was well-versed in scriptural studies and ascetics by the time he was introduced to Zen. He began to feel that these things were not yet the ultimate goal of the spiritual life.*

He was in one school of Buddhism which is based on *Vinaya Pitak*. Then the master himself, who must have been teaching him about *Vinaya Pitak*, about compassion and love and egolessness, simplicity, humbleness, the master must have introduced him to Zen.

He began to feel that these things were not yet the ultimate goal of the spiritual life.

And when he was introduced to Zen, he became aware that it was all good, but it was not the ultimate goal of the spiritual life. On the contrary it was a kind of programming, a cultivation of certain habits, character, a lifestyle—do this and don't do that. It was superficial.

Just today Amrito was telling me that a great scientist was asked, "Do you believe in God?" It seems obvious that the journalist who was asking this was a leftist atheist. He did not believe in God, and he could not conceive that a man of such a caliber, a great scientist, would say that he believes in God. The scientist said that he believed in God; the journalist was shocked. He said, "You are a great scientist and you still believe in God?"

The scientist said, "I have been programmed, it is not a question of my believing or not believing. I have been programmed from my very childhood that there is God—so continuously told by the parents, by the priests, by the teachers, everywhere, that it has become almost as if I know that God is. But it is only a conditioning."

All religions have been dependent on programming, not knowing exactly what programming is. The word is new in the world of psychologists, but the activity that has been done for centuries in the world by all the religions can be covered by this word 'programming'. The word came into existence with the computer. You have to program a computer. Whatever you want, you can put into the computer's mind. And it has a tremendous memory!

All the books that exist in the world, in all the libraries of the world, can be put into a computer. There is no need to waste so much space. Just one small computer can carry all the knowledge and you can ask it a question at any time, any absurd question—if it has been programmed. The programming has to be remembered. If it has been asked, "What was the day when Socrates was married?"— certainly it was an unfortunate day, but what was the day?—if the computer has been given the date and day, immediately the reply will come. Because of computers coming into existence, the word 'programming' has taken on tremendous meaning and implications.

What we are doing with computers, that is what religions have been doing with human beings. Somebody is a Hindu, and somebody is a Christian; what is the difference between the two? Just a different programming. If you bring up a Christian child from the very beginning in a Hindu household, do you think he will ever think about Jesus or about the Holy Bible? Will he ever ask questions that Christian children are bound to ask? He will be a Hindu because his programming will be Hindu. He will not even bother to waste time about Jesus. The same is true about all religions; every religion is programming the child, behaving with the child as if the child is a computer. It is the greatest insult to humanity and the greatest crime against every human being.

Every child comes with a clean slate. And then you start writing all over on it, the holy Bible, or holy Koran, or holy Gita, or holy *Das Kapital*—whatever you want. The poor child is in your hands, and he does not know yet and he cannot even think that his parents, who love him so much, will give him a wrong programming. But by the time he becomes aware of the word 'programming', the programming has gone to the very bones and marrow of the child. He cannot think otherwise.

Now in Europe and America, because many young people have deviated from the orthodox churches, a new kind of profession has come into being, the deprogrammer.

A child is no more interested in the old Bible, he does not go to the church, he becomes a hippie. He just goes against every norm that Christianity has been following. "Cleanliness is next to God"— and the hippie says there is no God and no cleanliness. It may be next, but neither of them exist. Just because the old society was insistent on cleanliness, the hippie has reacted, the youth has reacted against it.

Now with all kinds of reactions around the world, the fathers and the priests are very much worried, so they have asked psychoanalysts to create a system in which these people can be first deprogrammed, a continuous method of hypnotization, telling them, "You have gone astray. God is, and Jesus is his son. He is his only begotten son. And your religion is the highest and the greatest religion in the world." They put the person in a hypnotic sleep and they just go on repeating this. And it is a very simple thing to put a person into a hypnotic sleep; just tell him to gaze at anything that has radiating light. A candle will do; just concentrate on the candle and don't fall asleep and don't blink your eyes.

Naturally the eyes want to blink. Resist their natural tendency to blink, force yourself as much as possible to concentrate on the flame of the candle or anything that is shining enough and attracts your eyes. Within three to five minutes a person will have to fall asleep, because you cannot keep non-blinking eyes for more than three minutes; three minutes is the maximum.

When your eyes close automatically you cannot do anything

because they are tired enough and bored also. Just watching a flame cannot be much entertainment, it cannot be a very interesting experience. There is no juice in it, so you are bored, the eyes are tired, you are forcing them to keep open. And the hypnotist by your side goes on saying, "You are falling asleep, you are falling asleep," in a very sleepy voice. Soon you will find your eyes are closing and the hypnotist will be continuing, "Your eyes are becoming heavy, your lids are closing. You are going into a deep sleep."

It is a very simple method, but of profound significance. Once a person is just on the verge of falling asleep, the hypnotist says to him, "You will not hear anybody's voice except mine." And then the subject, the person, falls asleep, and he will not hear anything except the voice of the hypnotist. Now the hypnotist starts deprogramming him. If he has become a "Hare Krishna, Hare Rama," then he has to tell him, "It is all bullshit. You have gone away from your original great religion. You have gone away from Jesus." He will bring him back to Jesus.

So a double process is going on. On the one hand he is deprogramming the person from Hare Krishna, Hare Rama, and on the other hand he is reprogramming him to his old childhood programming. His Christianity is still there in his unconscious, so it is very easy to bring that unconscious to the surface. After a few sessions the Hare Krishna, Hare Rama has been completely forgotten. Now he knows it is all nonsense. He starts going to the church, he has come back to the right religion. But all that has happened is that his programming has been changed. Just anybody can put Hare Krishna, Hare Rama back.

My whole effort here is just to deprogram you and not to reprogram again; just to leave you as clean slates as when you were born, in your original nature, in your original face. Nowhere else is that being done. These people who are doing programming, deprogramming, reprogramming—they are all professionals, and the parents are paying them that their children should be brought back to the organized religion in which they were born.

My understanding is that birth has nothing to do with religion. Your parents may be Hindus or Christians, that does not mean that the child has to be a Hindu or a Christian. The child is not your possession. The child comes into the world through you. If you have any sense of humanity, any sense of respect, you will respect the child, and you will leave him alone and allow him to grow in his clarity, intelligence, in his inquiry for truth, even if he goes out of the fold in which you are programmed. If you love your child, let him go according to his nature, wherever it leads.

But no parent, no priest, is willing to give liberation to people, and everybody needs liberation from the priests. They are all against me for the simple reason that I am not a priest and I am not in favor of programming anybody.

My whole effort is to deprogram you so deeply that everything that has been put in you from your childhood is taken out and you are left again back in your childhood innocence. From that innocence begins your real journey of growth.

When Yakusan went to understand Zen, he immediately saw the difference. He was thinking while he was studying *Vinaya* that this is religion; but coming to the world of Zen, he saw that all that was nonessential. It is not the ultimate goal of life. That was really only programming, to tell you, "Be egoless, be compassionate, be loving to human beings, to living creatures." In Zen all these things will happen, not because of programming, but because of your own enlightenment, your own awareness, your own intensity and clarity. Compassion will come, but it will not be a cultivation. Love will come, but it will not be a parrot-like imitation.

Coming to the world of Zen he immediately realized that what he had been studying up to now was sheer wastage. It is not the ultimate goal. *He longed for true freedom and purity beyond the formulas of the dharma.* This is exactly what deprogramming means.

He longed for true freedom and purity beyond the formulas of the dharma. So, seeking guidance, he called on Sekitō.
Yakusan said to the master, "I have only a rough knowledge of three vehicles"—there are three scriptures and three schools in Buddhism—*"and the twelve branches of the spiritual teaching. But I hear that in the south there is a teaching about 'pointing directly at the mind of man and attaining buddhahood through the perception of the*

self-nature.' Now, this is beyond my comprehension. I humbly beseech you to graciously enlighten me on this."
Sekitō replied, "It is to be found neither in affirmation nor in negation, nor in affirming and negating at the same time. So what can you do?"
Yakusan was altogether mystified by these words.

I will have to tell you something so that you are not mystified by these words. In the West, Aristotle has given a logic which has only a dialectical process. Either something is negative or something is positive. In other words, either you believe in God or you don't believe in God. Yes and no—these two words are the foundation of Aristotelian logic.

But Buddha believes—and he is far more significant than Aristotle—he calls this twofold logic, "yes and no." If you ask Buddha if there is a God, he will say, "My first answer is yes, my second answer is no, my third answer is yes and no both." This he calls threefold logic.

It simply mystifies people—because what do you mean? Either you believe in God or you don't believe in God; twofold logic seems to be perfectly right. What is the point of threefold?

But he was not alone in this. His contemporary Mahavira had a sevenfold logic, and that is the last word, you cannot go beyond it— all possibilities, all angles. Yes and no are just two polarities, but you can be just in the middle. Yes and no both, or neither yes nor no— you can be just in the middle, not going to the extremes. And that was Buddha's way, known as the middle way.

Buddha says going to the extreme is wrong because you are choosing only one part; going to the other extreme is exactly in the same way wrong. Just be in the middle. The real is in the middle. But in the middle you cannot say yes, you cannot say no. Either you have to say both together, or you have to deny both together. That's what Sekitō is saying. Now hear it, and you will not be mystified by it.

"It is to be found," the truth has to be found, *"neither in affirmation,"* neither in saying yes, *"nor in negation,"* nor in saying no, *"nor in affirming and negating at the same time,"* nor in saying yes and no at the same time. Truth cannot be found in these three categories. The truth is beyond these three categories, it is the fourth. It is beyond logic, hence it cannot be expressed through any logical expression.

Poor Yakusan was at a loss. Even Sekitō asked him, "*So what can you do?* These are the three possibilities, none of them expresses the truth. What are you going to do?"

Yakusan was altogether mystified by these words. It seems he has come to the end of the road. *Hence, Sekitō told him frankly*—and this is the beauty of that golden milieu that has disappeared from the world—"*The cause and occasion of your enlightenment are not present here in this place. You should rather go to visit the great master, Ma Tzu.*"

Ma Tzu and Sekitō were the two opponent enlightened masters of that time. He is telling Yakusan to go to Ma Tzu although he is his opponent. "Your personality, your way of thinking...this place and the devices used here will not help you in growing up to your maturity. You should rather go to Ma Tzu. He will be a right atmosphere for you."

You can see the point. Sending a disciple to the opponent simply means that his interest is in the disciple and his growth, not in a growing following of his own. He looks at the person, feels his pulse, feels his heartbeat, and is clearly aware that "Here he will find it very difficult. Ma Tzu will be the right atmosphere for the man."

Following the suggestion, Yakusan went to pay his respects to Ma Tzu, presenting before him the same request as he had addressed to Sekitō. Ma Tzu replied, "I sometimes make him raise his eyebrows and turn his eyes; at other times I do not let him raise his eyebrows and turn his eyes. Sometimes it is really he who is raising his eyebrows and turning his eyes; at other times it is really not he who is raising his eyebrows and turning his eyes. How do you understand this?"

Yakusan must have been feeling he was almost going insane. Sekitō talked about logic and mystified him, and now this fellow is saying strange things. About whom is he talking?

At this, Yakusan saw completely eye-to-eye with Ma Tzu—seeing and listening to his words it became clear to him that there is something beyond the words. Sekitō has indicated towards it and now, listening to this man's almost crazy talk, one thing is certain, that truth cannot be explained in words. Both the masters have helped him to get rid of language. So rather than language, he *saw completely eye-to-eye with Ma Tzu and was enlightened. He bowed reverently to the master.*

Now just reading these words will not help, because something has happened which is not written and cannot be written. Something transpired when the disciple and the master looked into each other's eyes. In that silent moment some transmission, some energy... He has seen in the eyes of the master, "These are the eyes with which I can feel at ease. These are the eyes through which I can see the whole." It comes as an instantaneous, spontaneous realization, so nothing is said. That's what makes people worried about reading Zen.

Yakusan saw completely eye-to-eye with Ma Tzu and was enlightened. Now just reading this sentence will not explain anything unless you have seen into the eyes of a master, unless you have been in deep intimacy with a master, unless you have felt the presence and energy field of a master. It is a totally different universe, a totally different dimension of communicating, of communion.

He fell in love immediately. Those two eyes satisfied him absolutely: "This is the man I had been searching for for lives. I have come home." The realization was so tremendous and so strong that he became enlightened.

This is called in Zen "the transmission of the lamp." It is just as if you bring two candles close—one candle lighted, the other candle unlit. But bring them closer, and there is a point when suddenly the flame from one candle will jump to the other candle. Exactly something like that happens between a master and a disciple, when they encounter eye-to-eye. Yakusan became enlightened. Nothing has to be done.

What we are trying here is to bring your heart close to my heart, because that is the only way I can bring your heart to the universal heart. I am just a door to be passed, a bridge to be crossed.

An authentic master is not in any way a bondage to the disciple. He is simply a way, absolutely open and unconditional; you enter into him and through him you reach to the universe.

He bowed reverently to the master, who asked him, "What truth do you perceive that you should perform these ceremonies?"

Yakusan said, "When I was with Sekitō, I was like a mosquito crawling on a bronze ox."

Sekitō was a man—stoneheaded, a very hard shell. Yakusan says,

"I felt like a small mosquito crawling on a bronze ox. There was no way for me; I could not get into Sekitō, Sekitō was too hard."

Ma Tzu, discerning that the enlightenment was genuine, asked him to take good care of the insight. He attended upon Ma Tzu for three years. One day, Ma Tzu asked again, "What do you see recently?" Yakusan replied, "The skin has entirely moulted off; there remains only the one, true reality."

Ma Tzu said, "What you have attained is perfectly in tune with the innermost core of your mind, and from thence it has spread into your four limbs. This being the case, it is time to gird your waist with three bamboo splints, and go forth to make your abode on any mountain you may like."

Yakusan replied, "Who am I to set up any abode on any mountain?"

Ma Tzu said, "Not so! One cannot always be traveling without abiding, nor always be abiding without traveling. To advance from where you can no longer advance, and to do what can no longer be done, you must make yourself into a raft or ferryboat for others. It is not for you to abide here forever."

Ma Tzu was convinced that Yakusan had authentically become enlightened. Three years he had watched him, allowed him to be with himself. When it was certain, with all his gestures, activities, responses, that he had become a buddha, Ma Tzu told him, "Choose any mountain around, make your abode there."

He is telling him, "Now you are a master yourself, you need not be here. You have to become a ferryboat or a raft for others, those who want to go to the other shore. So make a temple, a monastery on some mountain, and those who are thirsty will come to you. You are not to be satisfied with your own enlightenment. That is very miserly. You have to spread the fire to those who are groping in the dark. You have to become a master of many who are blind. You have to give them eyes to see."

Ma Tzu is behaving exactly the way a buddha should behave on finding that another one has become a buddha. It is a wastage to keep him to himself. He should go now on his own, absolutely free to be himself, not to be under the shadow of a great master. It is almost like a gardener. He will remove a small plant from a big tree.

Underneath a big tree the small plant cannot grow. It needs its own space. It needs its own sun, its own sky, and once the gardener sees the potentiality of the plant—that it is not a weed but a rose—he takes it to an open sky where sun is available, fresh air is available, water is available.

Every master tries his best to give to his disciples independence, integrity, individuality, and a message—what you have gained, don't keep it to yourself. Share it. The more you share, the more you have it. The less you share, the less you have it. It is a different economics of the inner world. In the outer world the more you share it, the less you have it.

I have heard about a man who had just won a lottery, a million dollars. As usual he found the beggar standing by the side of the road. Today he was so happy, receiving one million dollars, he gave that beggar a one-hundred-dollar bill. The beggar looked at the bill, and he looked at the man, and he said to the man, "Soon you will be standing by my side."

He said, "What do you mean?"

The beggar said, "This is how I came to this state. I went on giving to everybody. Now I am in a state—I don't have anything, I have to beg. The way you are giving, it won't take much time. You can always come to me. I am an experienced beggar by now."

On the outside, in the objective world, there is one economics. You have to hold on to whatever you have, you have to cling to it. Not only you have to cling to your own, if you can manage to cling to others'…

George Bernard Shaw was asked once, "Can anyone live just keeping his hands in the pockets?"

George Bernard Shaw said, "Of course one can. But the pockets must be somebody else's."

In your own pockets you cannot live forever. In the objective world, if you share, you lose. But in the internal world just the opposite canon of thought is applicable. The more you share, the more you have; the less you share, the less you have. If you don't share at all, that small flame can disappear. By sharing it becomes a great fire. It consumes you.

A poem by Sōkō:

Inhale, exhale
forward, back,
living, dying:
arrows, let flown each to each,
meet midway and slice
the void in aimless flight—
thus I return to the source.

Go on throwing and throwing your experience, in life, in death.
Sōkō says, *thus I return to the source.* The more I give, the deeper I
reach to the source. It is just like digging a well. If you don't take out
the water from the well, the water will become dead. The more you
take the water out, the more fresh streams are opening up and bringing new water, fresh water from all sides.
Maneesha has asked a question:

Our Beloved Master,
If one has an authentic insight—not just an intellectual understanding
—it seems to take root and affect the way one is, of its own accord: noth-
ing needs to be done to preserve it.
Is this so? and is the situation different after enlightenment?

Maneesha, it is exactly as you describe it. If things start happening on their own accord, if you have found the source of your being,
that is the source of spontaneous happenings. Then you don't need
to preserve it, you don't need to guard it, you don't need to do
anything about it. It goes on happening.
Sharing also comes as a happening: because you are so flooded,
you are grateful to share. You are just like a raincloud; it needs to
rain. The rain is too heavy, it wants to unburden itself. So it is never
a problem of preserving it. Finding your life-source existentially, not
intellectually, you don't have to preserve it.
You are asking, "Is the situation different after enlightenment?"
After enlightenment one is no more. One becomes just a flute on

the lips of existence. Then existence is responsible for everything, a song or a silence. After enlightenment you are no more, only the existence is. Because you are no more, the other is also no more. For the other to be other, you have to be present. If you are absent, everybody is absent. That's why I say, when one person becomes enlightened, for him the whole existence becomes enlightened. Now there is no question of doing anything, not even sharing, because that is also doing.

It shares by itself.

It rains by itself.

Everything is now by itself.

Now it is Sardar Gurudayal Singh's time.

Blackie the dog walks into the Sizzling Salami Restaurant, and orders a tofu-burger.

"How would you like it cooked?" asks Sardar Gurudayal Singh, the waiter.

"I want it well done, with crushed cherries on top. Then fry some onions and put them on the side. Then get some peanut butter and put it all over it, then soak the whole thing in Coca-Cola."

Sardar Gurudayal Singh brings the food.

"Did you enjoy your dinner?" Sardar Gurudayal Singh asks, when the hungry hound is finished.

"Very much," replies the dog, licking his paws. "But, by the way, don't you think this is all very strange?"

"No," says Sardar Gurudayal Singh, grinning, "I like my tofu the same way!"

Bob and Betty are having a hot romance, and often go to the movies to cuddle in the back row.

One night when they are showing "Dracula and the Body Snatchers," and Dracula is about to sink his teeth into another Body Snatcher, Betty starts squealing and giggling.

The manager comes over, "What is the matter, young lady?" he asks, shining his light. "Are you feeling hysterical?"

"No," giggles Betty. "He is feeling mine!"

A man goes to apply for a job as janitor in a small office, and the boss asks him for his full name.

"What?" asks the man. "You need my full name just for a janitor's job?"

"Yes," replies the boss. "It is company policy."

The man is very shy about giving his full name, but finally agrees.

"All right then," he says, "my full name is John Dammit-and-Fuckit Smith."

The boss tries to keep a straight face, and then asks how he got such a name.

"Well," explains the man, "just as the bishop was about to christen me in the church, some idiot dropped the Holy Bible on his foot!"

Fudski is working on the forty-ninth floor of a new apartment construction, when he feels the need to pee.

"Is there a bathroom nearby?" he asks Luigi, the foreman.

"Listen," says Luigi, "with the wages we pay you, there is no time to go forty-nine floors down to get there. So do what everyone does: put a plank out over the edge. I'll stand on this end of the plank, and you walk to the other end and relieve yourself. By the time it reaches the ground, it will have evaporated."

"Great idea!" says Fudski.

He sets up the plank, Luigi stands on one end, and Fudski walks to the other end to pee.

Just then the phone rings, and Luigi goes to answer it. Poor Fudski goes sailing wildly through the air towards the ground below.

Luigi goes downstairs to see what has happened, but gets stopped on the way by Zabriski, who is working on the tenth floor.

"Hey!" shouts Zabriski, "what kind of perverts have you got on this job?"

"What do you mean?" asks a surprised Luigi.

"Well," replies Zabriski. "Some guy just came flying past here holding onto his prick and shouting, 'Where did that asshole go?'"

Nivedano...

Nivedano...

Be silent.
Close your eyes.
Feel your body to be completely frozen.
Look inside with immense urgency,
straight into your very center of being.
It is just a single step,
and your center is not only your center,
it is the center of the whole existence.

We are one at the center,
we are separate on the circumference.
Deeper and deeper,
go like an arrow,
finding the very life-source of your being,
that is also the life-source of all.
Remaining at the center,
just be a witness of your body, of your mind,
because this witness
is the only phenomenon in existence
that is eternal.
Everything dies.
Only this witness is beyond life and death.

Nivedano...

Relax,
and be a witness of the body and the mind.
You have not to do anything,
just watch, just be a mirror.
To be just an empty mirror with nothing reflected
is the greatest experience in life.
At this moment
you are in the same space as a buddha.
Inch by inch you are going deeper and deeper.
Soon the buddha will become
your twenty-four-hour experience.
It will express itself in your activities,

in your words, in your gestures,
in your silences, in your songs
and in your dances.
It will be at the very center
of all that you do, just watching.
But its watching will give a grace,
a tremendous beauty
to every action you do.
A great spontaneity will arise.
The same universe that you are acquainted with
will become tremendously beautiful.
Your witnessing will open all the doors
of mysteries and splendor.
This is a beautiful evening
and the gathering of ten thousand buddhas
makes it even more beautiful,
even more blissful, even more silent.
Invisible flowers are showering on you.
Gather as many as you can.
Soon you will be coming back,
but don't come back the same as you have gone in.
Come out transformed,
with a new light in your eyes,
with a new joy in your heart,
with a new sense of direction to your life.

Nivedano...

Come back,
but very silently and very gracefully.
Showing your buddha-nature,
sit down for a few moments
just remembering and recollecting,
you are a buddha.
Buddha is not somewhere else
but in the very center of your being.

Okay, Maneesha?
Yes, Beloved Master.
Can we celebrate the gathering of ten thousand
buddhas?
Yes, Beloved Master.

this
moment

Our Beloved Master,
A monk once drew four lines in front of Ma Tzu. The top line was long
and the remaining three were short. He then demanded of the master,
"Besides saying that one line is long and the other three are short, what else
could you say?"
Ma Tzu drew one line on the ground and said, "This could be called either
long or short. That is my answer."

On another occasion, a monk said to Ma Tzu, "What is the meaning of Bodhidharma's coming from the West?"

Ma Tzu replied, "At this moment, what do you mean by 'meaning'?"

Again the monk asked the question, and Ma Tzu struck him, saying, "If I didn't strike you, people would laugh at me."

E of Rokutan asked Ma Tzu the same question about Bodhidharma's coming from the West.

Ma Tzu said, "Lower your voice and come a little nearer!"

E went nearer. Ma Tzu struck him once, and said, "Six ears do not have the same plan. Come another day."

Later, E went to the hall and said, "I implore you to tell me!"

Ma Tzu said to him, "Go away for a time and come to the hall again when you have a chance, and I'll publicly confirm it."

E thereupon was enlightened. He said, "I thank everybody for their confirmation," and marched round the hall once, and went off.

On a later occasion, another monk said to Ma Tzu, "Please transcend the four sayings and refrain from the hundred negations, and tell me the meaning of Bodhidharma's coming from the West."

Ma Tzu said, "Today I'm tired and I can't tell you. Go and ask Chizō."

The monk went and asked Chizō, who said, "Why don't you ask the master?"

"He told me to come and ask you," said the monk.

"I've got an awful headache today," said Chizō, "so I can't tell you; go and ask Hyakujō."

The monk then went to Hyakujō, who said, "Well, as to that, I myself really don't know."

The monk reported all this to Ma Tzu, who said, "Hyakujō's cap is black; Chizō's cap is white."

Maneesha, before I discuss Ma Tzu and his statements, I have to inaugurate another god to Avirbhava's Museum of Gods. This is a very important god. I will tell you about the god before Avirbhava brings it in front of you.

The name of the god is horse. It has been worshipped around the world for centuries. Even today there are places where the horse is worshipped as a god.

"The horse or mare is one of the forms of the corn spirit in Europe.

"In Ancient Greece, Artemis and Aphrodite were associated with the horse, and Cronus is said to have taken the form of a horse.

"In Gaul, there was a horse goddess called Epona and a horse god called Rudiobus.

"The goddess mares, Medb of Tara and Macha of Ulster, were thought to have powers of the dead.

"Horse worship also existed in Persia, where white horses were regarded as holy. In the Teutonic regions they were kept in holy enclosures.

"Here, in India, in earlier times, horses were sanctified, and the cult exists still today. Koda Pen is the horse god of the Gonds."

In ancient India horses were not only worshipped, they were also sacrificed to please God. It was not only horses who were sacrificed; cows were killed, even man was killed as a sacrifice. For cows, the ritual was called *gomedh*—*go* means cow. For horses, the ritual was called *ashvamedh*. *Ashva* means horse, *medh* means killing. For man the ritual was called *naramedh*. *Nar* means man and *medh* means killing.

And these are the people who go on making a great fuss about stopping cow slaughter. They have slaughtered even man in the name of God. They themselves have slaughtered cows, horses, in the name of God. Sacrificing a living man in the name of God is very symbolic. To me it has more significance than just an ordinary sacrifice. The whole of humanity has been sacrificed by all the religions in the name of God.

You are living a crippled life because of the religions. They have not killed you, but they have not left you alive either. They have crippled you. They have cut you into parts. Certain parts in you have to be removed. Certain parts in you are worshipped, certain parts are condemned. Your wholeness is not accepted by any religion in the world. These religions are thought to be very intelligent, and they are worshipping animals of all kinds!

The first Hindu incarnation of God is the fish. Of course in Bengal, fish is eaten as something holy; rice and fish are their basic foods. The whole of Bengal stinks of fish. Every house has beautiful trees, even the poorest, and a beautiful pond in which they grow and cultivate fish. The scene is beautiful, very green. Nowhere is it so green as in Bengal, and every house has a pond, a big pond surrounded by big trees. You can know the riches of the family by the size of their pond. The richer families have vast ponds, and costly fishes are eaten in the name of God.

It is so easy to kill anything in the name of God. The name of God is a very protective shelter.

You will be surprised to know that when the Britishers came to India, they first captured Bengal, and Calcutta was their capital. Their first Indian servants, from the lowest to the highest, were all Bengalis. And because they were all stinking of fish, they started calling them "Babu." Babu is a Persian word which means a man who stinks. But because they were government servants, on high posts, "Babu" became very respectable. Now to call somebody Babu is very respectful, honorable.

The first president of India, Doctor Rajendra Prasad, was always called Babu Rajendra Prasad. And even that president had no idea that Babu is a dirty word. But people have forgotten the connotation. *Bu* means smell, and *ba* means really bad smell.

In Hinduism not only the fish was an incarnation of God. There was the tortoise, there was the pig, there was the lion, and a strange lion—half lion, half man—*narasinha*; the upper part of the body is of the lion, and the lower part of the body is of man. And people have worshiped them. One just wonders whether humanity is mad. Something is certainly insane.

And the last incarnation of God which is going to come is going to be a white horse. His name will be Kalki. And that white horse will save the virtuous and will destroy the sinners and will change the whole course of human history—a horse!

And all these idiots who believe in these things will be sitting by the side watching. The tenth incarnation of God is called Kalki. He is to come to judge the world at the end of this yuga, the fourth and last cycle of one million, eight hundred thousand years in the Hindu concept of the world. He will destroy the wicked, reward the good, and enable Vishnu, the Hindu God, to create a new world.

In Buddhism, the horse represents the indestructible, the hidden nature of things. The winged or cosmic horse, called "Cloud," is a form of Avalokiteshvara. It is an incarnation of Gautam Buddha.

I am allowing these animal gods in this campus to make you aware of your past. And it is not passed completely, it is still hidden in your mind.

In Varanasi...it is a strange place, it is the ancientmost city in the world. Because of its being so ancient its streets are very small, because in those days there was no need for buses and trucks and cars to move. Even a rickshaw hardly manages to move through the streets.

It is thought to be a great virtue to take an ox and leave it in the city of Varanasi. The city of Varanasi is thought to be the city of the God Vishnu, and he loves cows. So in the city of Varanasi you will find more cows than men, and you cannot remove a cow that is standing in the street. You go on honking your horn and those gods are not going to listen to such ordinary human beings. Go on honking...they will just stand there without bothering.

You have to get down and push them to the side. You cannot hit them otherwise you will be killed. It will be hurting the Hindu religious feelings. They enter into shops, into vegetable shops, and they start eating. You cannot stop them. They are no ordinary people, they are VVIPs!

Varanasi, in the whole world...

(At this moment ripples of laughter spread through the assembly as a white horse enters the auditorium through the door to the left of the podium, gallops around it and disappears through the door on the right.)

So, Avirbhava, you can come back, your horse is introduced. Come back to your seat.

(Great applause from the audience.)

Now, Maneesha's statements about Ma Tzu and his work:
Ma Tzu was one of the first masters to use a specifically Zen technique in teaching; that is, through living, not philosophical ideas. By indicating the absolute in the relative—a relative without religious dogma, romance, symbolism, or intellectualism, but with a deep sense of the existential value of a thing—Ma Tzu brought Zen into the realm of ordinary, day-to-day living.

His contribution to Zen is immense. He brought it down from the heights to where you are. About Ma Tzu it can be said, just as it is said about Mohammed... Mohammed is reported to have said that if the thirsty will not come to the well, the well is going to go to the thirsty.

To go to the heights of buddhas is really an arduous thing. They shine forth like a full moon in the sky, and a tremendous longing arises in you to reach to the same heights. But there is a great fear of insecurity, of danger, of those mountainous regions where you will be alone. Many who want to reach to those heights think twice before they take their first step.

Ma Tzu saw this and he introduced something which was never known before. He came down from the mountains to the marketplace. He said, "The marketplace cannot change me, so why avoid it? I am going to change the marketplace. Sitting on my heights, I will not be able to change thousands of people. And if when it is possible I go to the people themselves, just as ordinary as they are, communication will be easier."

Hence he dropped all philosophical teachings. He brought new devices, more in tune with the earth, not in tune with the sky, more in tune with the ordinary human activities. Once he has got hold of you, he will take you to the heights. But the first question is to take hold of you.

He is the first master in the history of Zen who has shown such compassion. He also introduced beating for the first time. That too is part of his compassion. His beating has to be understood because it will come again and again. He is beating you to wake you up. There is no need to go anywhere to find the buddha. The buddha is fast asleep within you. He just needs a little awakening. The beating was out of pure love and compassion.

It is very difficult for other religions in the world to understand: "What kind of teaching is this? Teach about God, teach about heaven and hell and virtues and ten commandments." To them it will look ...it does look almost crazy.

But Ma Tzu helped far more people to become enlightened than any other master. The end result shows that his devices worked.

A monk once drew four lines in front of Ma Tzu. The top line was long and the remaining three were short. He then demanded of the master, "Besides saying that one line is long and the other three are short, what else could you say?"

Ma Tzu drew one line on the ground and said, "This could be called either long or short. That is my answer."

It reminds me of an incident in a court of a great Indian emperor, Akbar. One day he came into the court and drew a line on the wall and told all the members of his court...and he had collected the most wise people from all parts of the country into his court; it must have been the richest court in the world as far as wisdom is concerned. He had all the great artists, musicians, dancers—anybody who was at the top was invited to be part of his court.

He asked the court members, "Can you make this line smaller without touching it?" It looks like a Zen koan. How can you make it smaller without touching it? You will have to touch it, only then you can make it smaller. That seems to be obvious.

But one man laughed. He was the court joker, Birbal. Every court in the ancient days used to have a court joker, just to keep the court playful, nonserious. There were serious problems, but the joker would always keep it cool; he would cut a joke, and all the heat would disappear, and people would come to their senses. Birbal perhaps is one of the most well known men, who had an immense sense of humor; but he was also a wise man. He stood up and he went to the wall and drew a bigger line above the small line that Akbar had drawn. And he said, "I have made it small without touching it"—because small, or long, or short, are all relative terms.

In itself you can draw a line...that's what Ma Tzu is doing, drawing a line. And he says, "You can call it either long or short." It is a question of relativity. If you are comparing it with a longer line, it is short; if you are comparing it with a shorter line, it is long. In itself it is just what it is. Relativity is a comparison with something else.

Why Ma Tzu did it has to be understood. And particularly now that Albert Einstein has introduced the theory of relativity in the scientific sphere, it has become more important to understand Ma Tzu's meaning. He is saying, "Everyone is just himself, neither great nor small—because that greatness or smallness comes from relativity —neither beautiful nor ugly. Everyone is simply just himself."

You can bring a taller man by his side and he becomes smaller, but *he* remains the same. Only relatively, conceptually, intellectually, can you see that he is smaller, but he has not changed even an inch. You can bring a pygmy by his side and suddenly he has become taller, and he has not changed a bit. What he is saying is that relativity is a dangerous concept to be applied to human beings.

It is relativity that makes some people big, great, famous, celebrities. Some people live in obscurity, some people are just nobodies. This is relativity; otherwise everybody is just himself, it does not make any difference. There is no question of inequality, everybody is unique. The person who is nobody is happy in his nobodiness. But this concept of relativity drives people mad. Everybody is trying to climb higher on the ladder, to become somebody special. And even the most special people are hankering for so many things which they are missing.

For example, Napoleon was one of the world conquerors. But he was suffering from a great inferiority complex because of his height —he was only five feet five inches tall. Even his bodyguards were over six feet and he felt very much embarrassed—on both sides bodyguards, and bodyguards are chosen particularly to be strong, tall. He looked just like a small child in comparison to his own bodyguards, and this was very embarrassing.

One day he was trying to fix a picture on the wall, but his reach was just a little bit short, he could not reach the picture. His body-guard said, "Your honor, you need not bother about it. I am higher than you, I can do it without any difficulty."

Napoleon said, "I will shoot you. Change your word 'higher'. You are simply taller than me, not higher."

The poor bodyguard could not see why he had become so angry. He had touched the very soft spot in his unconscious. Higher?—nobody is higher. At the most you can say, physiologically, that you are taller. But Napoleon suffered immensely. Every time he saw a taller man, he was in immense misery.

You cannot have all the things in the world. There will be poets, there will be musicians, whose very touch is golden. There will be wrestlers whose bodies are almost a work of art. You cannot have all these things. Relatively, everybody is inferior in comparison to some-body else. You can find out to whom you are inferior, and you will find so many people to whom you are inferior. Somebody is a great flutist and you don't know which side of the flute to put in your mouth. Somebody is a great mathematician...miraculous mathematicians have happened.

In India, just in this century, there were two people; one was Shankaran, a rickshaw wallah in Madras. Just by chance a professor in the Madras university took his rickshaw and on the way the rick-shaw wallah asked him, "What do you teach in the university?"

He was an Englishman. He said, "I am a professor of mathematics."

The rickshaw wallah said, "Mathematics? That is my special subject. You just tell me any number, multiplied by any other number, and before you have ended your question I will answer it." And he did it.

The professor could not believe his own eyes and ears. The number that he had given to be multiplied by another number would have taken the greatest mathematician at least three minutes. Without going through the whole process, he had simply answered. And the professor had to work it out, whether his answer was right or wrong—and it was right.

He took him to the university. Shankaran convinced all the professors that he had an intuitive grasp. Asked how he managed it, he said he did not know. "Just as you ask, a number appears on the screen of my mind, and I simply repeat that number. I don't know any process, I am not educated."

The professor took him around the world as a show of intuitive mathematics—to Oxford, to Cambridge—and everywhere he was a celebrity. An uneducated rickshaw wallah—and great mathematicians like Whitehead, Bertrand Russell, they simply could not believe it.

Bertrand Russell has written the greatest book on mathematics. Just to explain two plus two is four, he has taken two hundred and forty pages. And this man—you give him any number to multiply or any kind of question, and he immediately writes the answer on the board. He goes through no process.

And then there is another woman, her name is Shakuntala, and I think she is still alive—and strangely from the same place, Madras. She has been around the world showing her intuitive capacity for mathematics.

Even great mathematicians have felt childish next to these people; they are not educated, they know nothing of mathematics, but they can make the greatest mathematicians feel inferior.

If you are going to compare, if you are going to think around, you will find thousands of people who will make you inferior. And you cannot do anything about it. You cannot be the greatest dancer, you cannot be the greatest mathematician, you cannot be the greatest poet, you cannot be the greatest painter; you cannot have all the greatness in the world at the same time.

The very idea of thinking in relativity about human beings is absurd. You are just yourself. Just be authentically yourself, without any comparison. No inferiority arises; no superiority arises. You are simply relaxed as you are. And whatever you are doing, you do your best, with joy and creativity.

Ma Tzu's answer...he *drew one line on the ground and said, "This could be called either long or short. That is my answer."*

It depends with what you are comparing it. But why compare in the first place?

Relativity is perfectly good in scientific fields. It is absolutely wrong in the world of humanity. Human beings are not mathematical digits; human beings are unique. Everyone—however he is, whatever he is—has just to bring his potentiality to its totality, its profundity, to clean it and bring it to blossom. It does not matter whether it is a wildflower or a roseflower. What matters is flowering, bringing your potentiality to its uttermost height.

And that will bring you joy and peace, and a rest, a relaxation with the universe. You will be in tune, and there will be no turmoil in your mind—how to become this, how to become that. How to be the richest person, how to be the most famous—all that is garbage; and it is driving thousands of people mad, unnecessarily mad.

They could be the most beautiful people if they were not thinking in terms of relativity. If they were satisfied with themselves and their potential, and they were working to bring their potential to its uttermost height, without any comparison to anyone—this is the only way a man can be psychologically healthy.

On another occasion, a monk said to Ma Tzu, "What is the meaning of Bodhidharma's coming from the West?"

This is a traditional question in Zen, asked thousands of times, asked to hundreds of different masters by thousands of disciples; and every time a different answer.

Ma Tzu is not going to give any philosophical answer.

The philosophically oriented masters can give much meaning to Bodhidharma's coming from India to China—remember that in China, India is the West.

Bodhidharma brought Gautam Buddha's message, and he transformed the whole of China into a great love affair with Buddha. He did not create an organized religion, he simply spread the fragrance of Buddhism. No organized church, but everybody is allowed to drink from the well of Buddha, and quench his thirst. No priest exists in Buddhism—there is no need of the priest. He is a hindrance, not a bridge. You can be a buddha yourself, just by going within yourself. No priest is needed for that.

China was so happy to hear the message, "You are a buddha; you just don't understand your interiority, your subjectivity."

So much can be said about *"What is the meaning of Bodhidharma's coming from the West?"*

But *Ma Tzu replied, "At this moment, what do you mean by 'meaning'?"*

Ma Tzu was a strange master with strange methods. Rather than answering the question, he turns the question into another question. He changes the whole thing.

He asks, *"At this moment, what do you mean by 'meaning'?"*

Again the monk asked the question, and Ma Tzu struck him, saying, "If I didn't strike you, people would laugh at me."

A strange anecdote, but Ma Tzu is right. He is saying, "The whole meaning of Gautam Buddha and his message is *you*. Bodhidharma came here to wake you up. Rather than philosophizing about it, I will do exactly the same as Bodhidharma did.

At this moment, what do you mean by 'meaning'?"

That comes as a shock, because the monk was not thinking that somebody would ask this question.

Again the monk asked the question, and Ma Tzu struck him, saying, "If I didn't strike you, people would laugh at me—because you are the meaning, and you are asking it. You are the buddha, and you are asking where the buddha is. If I don't strike you, for centuries people will laugh about me."

E of Rokutan asked Ma Tzu the same question about Bodhidharma's coming from the West.

Ma Tzu said, "Lower your voice and come a little nearer!"

E went nearer. Ma Tzu struck him once, and said, "Six ears do not have the same plan. Come another day."

The man could not understand. He is asking a traditionally simple question, "What was the meaning of Bodhidharma's coming to China?" And Ma Tzu is answering it in two ways: first, "Lower your voice!"

The man must have asked as if the answer is not possible. The man must have asked with a great ego, expecting that Ma Tzu is going to accept defeat.

Saying to him, "Lower your voice!" simply means, "Be quiet, be silent, be humble, because in your humbleness you will find the answer; in your silence you will find the meaning."

And, "Come a little nearer!" The man did not understand the meaning of coming a little nearer. He is saying, "Be a little more intimate with me, come a little closer to my heart, be a little more open. Don't just stand there closed, and with a great ego. Be humble and come closer."

But he did not understand the meaning either of lowering the voice, or of coming a little nearer. He went nearer—physically.

Ma Tzu struck him once, and said, "Six ears do not have the same plan. Come another day—you have not understood today, but who knows?—*Come another day.* It is enough for today that I have given you a good hit. Think over it."

And *"Six ears do not have the same plan."*

Here you are thousands of ears, but behind your ears everybody has a different plan. So come another day and drop your plan. If you come with a prejudice, with an answer already within you, you cannot understand me.

Here we don't work philosophically. This is not the place for intellectuals. For that you can go anywhere, to any monastery where scriptures are thought to lead you to your inner nature. But if you want to hear the answer from me, come another day. For today it is enough.

Later, E went to the hall and said, "I implore you to tell me!"
Ma Tzu said to him, "Go away for a time and come to the hall again when you have a chance, and I'll publicly confirm it."
E thereupon was enlightened. He said, "I thank everybody for their confirmation," and marched round the hall once, and went off.

Everything around Ma Tzu is very mysterious. The man did not go, he followed Ma Tzu to the assembly hall. And again in the assembly hall he repeated it, but now, just within a few moments, he was a different person. He said, *"I implore you to tell me!"*

That old egoist of a few moments before is no longer there. The voice has become one of imploring, of humbleness.

Ma Tzu said to him, "Go away for a time and come to the hall again when you have a chance, and I will publicly confirm it."

He has not given the answer, but he has given something else. He is asking him to go away, "and come here only when you have a chance of getting the answer. That means when you have meditated over it, dropped all your preconceptions, when you don't have any idea what is the answer. That will be your chance. Then you can come, *and I will publicly confirm it.*"

Because he has asked with humbleness, the man must have been of great intelligence. Time does not make any sense; why not do it now? So he dropped—that is not written in the anecdote, that cannot be written, it is something that is happening within him—he dropped all his notions. And as he dropped all his notions, there was no need for any answer for him.

It is a strange situation. When the question disappears, there is no need for the answer either. That is all mental gymnastics. Seeing the truth, that the master is not going to get involved in intellectual conversation... Perhaps there is no way to intellectually explain the meaning of Bodhidharma's coming to the West. It is something that can be transmitted only when you are utterly silent and without any questions. Then a flame, a fire can jump from the master's heart. And that actually happened.

E thereupon was enlightened. He said, "I thank everybody for their confirmation," and marched round the hall once, which is a sign of reverence, *and went off.*

On a later occasion, another monk said to Ma Tzu, "Please transcend the four sayings and refrain from the hundred negations, and tell me the meaning of Bodhidharma's coming from the West."
Ma Tzu said, "Today I'm tired and I can't tell you. Go and ask Chizō." Chizō was one of his nearest disciples.
The monk went and asked Chizō, who said, "Why don't you ask the master?"
"He told me to come and ask you," said the monk.
"I've got an awful headache today," said Chizō, "so I can't tell you; go and ask Hyakujō." Hyakujō was the second most intimate disciple of Ma Tzu.
The monk then went to Hyakujō, who said, "Well, as to that, I myself really don't know."

The monk reported all this to Ma Tzu, who said, "Hyakujō's cap is black; Chizō's cap is white."

Now the question is completely forgotten. Nobody has answered it. On the contrary, Hyakujō has accepted that he himself does not know what the answer is.

The white cap and the black cap refer to an old story of two robbers. One of the robbers wore a white cap, while the other wore a black cap. As the story goes, the one with the black cap was more ruthless and radical than the one with the white. So it was that Hyakujō was said to be more radical than Chizō in his methods of dealing with young monks.

Ma Tzu said that he was very tired. *"Today I am tired and I can't tell you."* The fact is, whether you are tired or not, you *can't* tell it. The meaning of Bodhidharma is an experience, it is not an explanation. But to be humble, Ma Tzu did not say, "Nothing can be said about it." On the contrary, he took the whole responsibility on himself. *"Today I'm tired and I can't tell you. Go and ask Chizō."*

He took this opportunity also to check upon Chizō and Hyakujō. He knew that Chizō would not be able to answer, neither would Hyakujō. This question in Zen is one of those unanswerable things which can only be experienced. There is no way to bring them to words. The man went to Chizō, who said, "Why don't you ask the master? Why bother me? I am just a disciple."

But the monk said, *"He told me to come and ask you...."*

"I've got an awful headache today," said Chizō, *"so I can't tell you; go and ask Hyakujō."*

The monk then went to Hyakujō, who said, "Well, as to that, I myself really don't know."

The monk reported all this to Ma Tzu, who said, "Hyakujō's cap is black; Chizō's cap is white."

That is referring to the story of those two robbers. The robber who used to use the black cap was a radical revolutionary. And Ma Tzu says that Hyakujō's cap is black. It is a tremendous statement to say that you don't know, it needs guts to accept your ignorance. Chizō's cap is white. He is trying to hide—as if he knows, but because he has a great headache, today he cannot say it.

Ma Tzu worked in strange ways. Now he has worked with a single question on three persons: on the monk who has brought the question, on Chizō, who is trying to hide his ignorance, on Hyakujō, who comes out with his radical answer, "I don't know."

"I don't know" is the greatest answer in the whole experience of humanity.

Socrates said, "I don't know," at the very last moment of his life. His whole life he was teaching the truth, and at the last moment he said, "I don't know." At the last moment he becomes really humble, and he sees the greatness of truth and its miraculousness, its inexpressibility—and that what he had been doing was just playing with words all his life. Now, no more; he is going to die within a few minutes. The poison is being prepared. At least the world should know that Socrates, before dying, uttered his honest answer, "I don't know. I don't know anything about anything. I am just as innocent and ignorant as a child."

But this is the highest peak of wisdom. When you don't know, the mind is empty, you have arrived at the empty heart. When you know, the mind is full. Knowledge is the greatest barrier in reaching to the universal, to the immortal, to the eternal truth. Knowledge is the greatest barrier, which is preventing you from recognizing your buddha-nature.

Chizō was closer to Ma Tzu but he did not get the succession. Hyakujō was chosen to be the successor. When Ma Tzu died…before dying he declared Hyakujō. Nobody was expecting that; everybody knew that Chizō would be the successor. But Hyakujō was chosen for the simple reason that he had the guts to express his ignorance, his innocence.

The statement "I don't know," is the greatest statement anybody can make. It makes your heart completely empty. Here in our meditations we are doing exactly this. My whole effort is to take away all your knowledge, because it is all borrowed, and unnecessarily you are carrying it. It does not allow your heart to be empty, and only an empty heart is capable of falling in tune with the universal heart. From that point life becomes a celebration.

Sōseki wrote,

This piece of wild land
has no boundaries—
north, south, east or west.
It is hard to see even the tree
in the middle of it.
Turning your head
you can look beyond each direction.
For the first time you know that your eyes
have been deceiving you.

When you go inwards there is no east, no west, no south, no north; just pure space, in all directions the same. You have gone to your very roots, and now you know for the first time that all these many lives your eyes have been deceiving you because they were keeping you attached to the objects of the outside. They were not allowing you to enter into yourself. You were kept engaged in something outside—money, knowledge, respectability.

There are thousands of ways to keep you engaged so that you don't turn inwards. Life is being managed by the society in such a way that from the very beginning you are forced to remain engaged. It becomes a habit. If you don't have anything to do, you find something to do. I know people...on Sundays they are in the most uncomfortable position—nothing to do! They may open an old grandfather clock to repair it—it was working already. Or they may go to the car and open the bonnet, and the car is functioning perfectly well—but it is something to do. They may read the same newspaper again.

I used to live with a relative for a few days. He was retired and he used to read the same newspaper from the morning till the night. And I would say, "How many times do you read your newspaper?"

He said, "It is not a question of reading. The question is that I have nothing to do. My wife is dead. She used to keep me engaged—'Bring this, bring that'—and she used to nag me. Now I miss her so much. At that time I used to think that it would be good if she died because she was a pain in the neck. But at least there was something to be engaged in. Now I am utterly useless."

Here you all know Maitreya who is lying in his *samadhi*. He used

147

to keep all the newspapers—old newspapers. Once I looked into his room. I could not go into his room because he used to eat garlic so much that the whole room was stinking with garlic. He has been connected with me for almost forty years. He has been a member of the parliament. He always asked me to stay with him in his house in Delhi, and I always said, "No. Until you drop your garlic there is no way. I cannot enter your house."

He said, "It is very difficult for me to drop the garlic. I can drop everything"—and he dropped everything: he dropped his wife, he dropped his house, he dropped his membership of the parliament, he became a sannyasin—but garlic, that he could not manage. So I never entered into his room—he lived with me in my own house— just from the outside of the door I would have a look at how many old papers...they were going almost to the ceiling. And I asked him, "What are you going to do with these old newspapers? Are you mad or something?"

And he would laugh and he would say, "Sometimes, when one has nothing to do, it is perfectly good to read some old newspapers. It is just an old politician's habit."

His constituency was Patna. In Patna he insisted very much that I should stay in his home. I said, "I can stay in a hotel. But even if my life is at risk, I will not enter into your house. Garlic I cannot tolerate. It is so dangerous, the very smell." When he died, I said, "My God, it is good. At least now nobody will be bringing garlic into this house!"

And I have said that now nobody should be allowed to stay in my house who is a fan of garlic—and there are fans! This Sarjano, making all kinds of spaghetti, is a garlic fan. It is good that the government of Italy does not allow me to enter into Italy. I am so happy about it. And my sannyasins, Sarjano, Majid, and others, they go on forcing the parliament and I am much worried that someday...

For two years continuously the parliament has been discussing it. Finally they agreed to give me a three-week visa, with conditions. That was very good. I refused; I refused completely. "With conditions I cannot enter into your country. Remove all conditions, then I will consider it." So the government is still considering, and I hope that they will not allow me because I am certainly worried that the whole

of Italy must be stinking of garlic. I know so many Italian sannyasins
—I keep them a little far away.

Maneesha has asked:

Our Beloved Master,
I don't know the meaning of Bodhidharma's coming from the West, but
there does seem to be a significance in his taking the existential religion of
Zen to the East, and You—so many centuries later—bringing it back again
to contemporary man. Through the two of you, Zen has made a full circle.
Are You in partnership with Bodhidharma?

Maneesha, that is an open secret.

It is Sardar Gurudayal Singh's time.

Sardar Gurudayal Singh has a new job as a waiter in the swank
Ken's House of Pancakes. Two gentlemen have just finished their
dinner, and Sardar Gurudayal Singh approaches them.

"Tea or coffee, gentlemen?" asks Sardar Gurudayal Singh.

"I will have tea," says the first man.

"Yes, I will also have tea," says the second, "but make certain the
glass is clean."

A few minutes later, Sardar Gurudayal Singh returns and says,
"Here we are, two teas. Now, which one of you gentlemen asked for
the clean glass?"

Doctor Feelgood is at a psychiatrists' convention in New York.
During one of the breaks he goes into the cafeteria. He notices a
beautiful woman sitting alone in the corner, drinking coffee. She is
so beautiful and attractive that Feelgood cannot resist the temptation
to talk to her.

He goes up close to her and asks quietly, "Can I join you?"

The young lady shrink looks at him for a few seconds and then
replies, "Why, do I look like I'm falling apart?"

Get it now?

Walter and Larry, two Australian boundary riders, are drinking beer and discussing how smart their dogs are.

"My dog Rex is so smart," says Walter, "that I can give him five instructions at once and he will carry them out, one by one."

"That's nothing!" replies Larry. "My dog Butch just needs one instruction from me, and then he anticipates the rest."

After a few more beers, Walter whistles for Rex. He tells him to run down the street, turn left at the traffic lights, go half a mile and bring back a black sheep from the field there.

Ten minutes later, Rex is back with the sheep.

"Not bad," says Larry, "but watch this!" Then he calls to Butch.

"Butch," says Larry, "I am hungry!"

Butch races away down the road until he sees a chicken shed. He digs a hole under the fence, lifts a hen off its nest, and picks up an egg from underneath it.

Then he races back to Larry, puts down the egg, picks up a small pot, races off to fetch some water, puts the pot on the fire and then drops the egg in.

Exactly three minutes after the water boils, Butch tips out the water, picks up the egg, delivers it to Larry and then stands on his head with his tail in the air.

"That is incredible!" says Walter, "but tell me—why is he standing on his head like that, with his ass in the air?"

"Well, he's a smart dog," replies Larry. "He knows that I don't have an egg cup."

Nivedano...

Nivedano...

Be silent.
Close your eyes.
Feel your body to be completely frozen.
Look inwards with great urgency.
You have to reach, this very moment,
to your center.
Your center is your eternity.
The moment you are at the center,
you are just a witness—
a mirror that reflects the body, the mind,
but knows perfectly well it is utterly empty.
The empty mirror...
and the doors of all the mysteries of existence
open for you.
Deeper and deeper...
Make this evening a milestone in your life.
Recognize your buddha

and then act it out twenty-four hours,
round the clock—
in every gesture, in every activity,
peacefully, gracefully,
with a watching heart, silently.
This is the very essence of religion;
all other things are only
nonessential commentaries.
The word witness contains all the scriptures.

Nivedano...

Make it clear that you are not the body, nor the mind,
but just the watching consciousness,
the witness.
The evening is great,
and your silence has made it greater.
It is so beautiful,
and your witnessing has added
immense beauty to it.
On the whole earth at this moment, this place,
where ten thousand people are simply witnessing,
has a unique character.
In the past, many places like this used to be.
Unfortunately, those golden days are past,
but my effort is to bring those golden moments again
in the future of humanity.
You are going to be the vehicles.

Nivedano…

Come back…
but come back as a buddha,
without any hesitation,
without any doubt.
This is the only trust I teach.
You are the buddha.
Sit down for a few moments,
just to recollect the whole experience.
The rains have come to welcome you.
What a splendor, this moment.
What a silence, this moment.

Okay, Maneesha?
Yes, Beloved Master.
Can we celebrate the ten thousand buddhas?
Yes, Beloved Master.

Our Beloved Master,

On one occasion, a monk called on Ma Tzu and asked him, "Who is the man who does not take all dharmas as his companions?"

Ma Tzu replied, "I will tell you this after you have swallowed all the water in the West River."

Upon hearing this, the monk was instantaneously awakened, and he stayed for two years at Ma Tzu's monastery.

no ripples

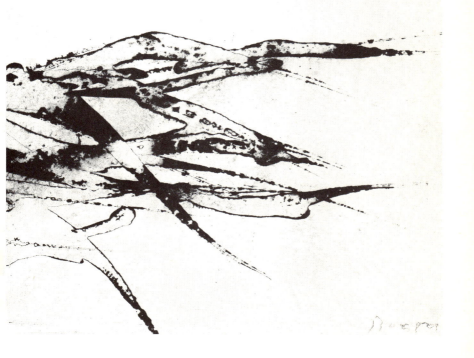

At another time, Ma Tzu said, "Every dharma is the dharma of the mind, and every name is a name of the mind. All beings are born of the mind, and so mind is the foundation of all beings.

"As an example: the shadow of the moon reflected on the water has many shapes, but the real moon is not like that. Likewise there are various rivers, but the nature of the water is the same. Although there are myriad activities, there is no discrimination in the emptiness. Different things go through the different ways, but the liberated wisdom is one. All are based on one mind.

"Every dharma is based on the dharma of Buddha. Each dharma is instantly the dharma of realization, and the dharma of realization is, things being as they really are.

"All that come and go and have a rest, or sit and lie down, are the mysterious work, and they don't need a process of time. The scriptures also say: 'All around everywhere, instantaneously there are buddhas.'"

Ma Tzu continued, "Cultivation is of no use for the attainment of Tao. The only thing that one can do is to be free of defilement. When one's mind is stained with thoughts of life and death, or deliberate action, that is defilement. The grasping of the truth is the function of everyday-mindedness.

"Everyday-mindedness is free from intentional action, free from concepts of right and wrong, taking and giving, the finite or the infinite.... All our daily activities—walking, standing, sitting, lying down—all response to situations, our dealings with circumstances as they arise: all this is Tao."

maneesha, care of Anando.... She *is* here—where else can she be? But she is hiding behind a migraine. You have to remember yesterday's anecdote. Master Ma Tzu was hiding behind tiredness: "I am too tired to answer this question today. You go to Chizō." The reality was that the question could not be answered. Chizō said, "I am suffering from severe headache. It is better you go to Hyakujō." Hyakujō simply gave up the secret; he simply said, "I don't know."

The reason for Maneesha's migraine is the question she has asked. When we come to the question, you will understand why she has a migraine.

The story she has brought:

On one occasion, a monk called on Ma Tzu and asked him, "Who is the man who does not take all dharmas as his companions?"

Ma Tzu himself was the man who had said, "I am only the witness. All dharmas are just objects, I witness them. For example: compassion arises in me—I am not compassion. I can see it arising just like smoke arises out of fire, or flames arise out of fire. But I am not it."

Any dharma, any virtue, is as objective as anything else in the world. Only one thing is not objective in the world, and that is your very being—your witnessing self. It can never be made into an object; it is impossible to reduce it to an object. It will always remain the witness and can never become the witnessed.

Except this, you cannot say anything more about it. And because it is not attached to any dharma, any attribute, it has an eternal life, it has an immortality, and it has a reach into the very depths of the universe.

Ma Tzu was himself the man. The monk was asking Ma Tzu, *"Who is the man who does not take all dharmas as his companions?"*

He must be angry, because there are other Buddhist schools which say that all the dharmas belong to the self. Compassion, love, truth—all the dharmas are attributes of your being, branches of your own being, flowers of your own being. And this is a far bigger majority opinion.

Ma Tzu is unique in his understanding that only one thing—witnessing—is the nature of your being. Everything else that can be witnessed falls separate from you. It becomes the other. The moment it is objectified, it becomes the other.

The man must have been in anger when he asked this.

Ma Tzu replied, "I will tell you this after you have swallowed all the water in the West River."

Seeing his anger, rather than answering him, Ma Tzu said, "Just go to the river, and swallow all the water of the river. Even that much water may not be able to quench your anger. Then come back, and I will answer you."

Upon hearing this, the man suddenly must have become aware of his anger. That is the whole teaching of Zen. Whichever school one belongs to, watching is unavoidably part of the discipline.

Suddenly he must have become aware that he has asked the question not out of a quest, but out of anger. He calmed down. Suddenly a tremendous coolness came to him, as if he had already swallowed the whole river.

Upon hearing this, the monk was instantaneously awakened, and he stayed for two years at Ma Tzu's monastery.

Enlightenment is a question of a sudden realization—that you are neither anger, nor greed, nor love, nor compassion. Anything that you can name, you are not. You are the unnameable witness, hidden deep inside you, just reflecting everything that passes by, just a mirror.

I have called this series *Ma Tzu: The Empty Mirror* for the simple reason that his whole teaching is: don't react—just be, and reflect. Clouds will come and go, and the sky remains as empty as ever. Clouds don't leave any mark on the empty sky. And just as outside there is this vast empty sky—it is immeasurable—on the other side, inwards, the same infinity exists. You are standing just in the middle between an outer infinity and an inner infinity. You can go in either direction—outwards, and you will not find any limit, or inwards, and you will not find any limit.

Science has been struggling for three hundred years, because it was determined that there must be a boundary line to the universe. To the mind it is not appealing, it seems irrational that something can be without boundaries. How can it be without boundaries? The boundaries may be millions of miles away, millions of light years away; but that does not matter, it still remains limited.

But finally, with Albert Einstein, science accepted its failure. Now we have immensely powerful instruments to find the farthest star, but even the farthest star is not the limit. Albert Einstein accepted it humbly that, rational or irrational—what can we do?—existence is unlimited. If anything, we can change our logic and rationality, but we cannot change the universe.

The inward infinity is far more mysterious, just because it is more alive. The deeper you go, the deeper you are going into life, into abundant life. And the deeper you go, you find only one quality, that of the mirror. You reflect everything, and nothing affects you.

Only at this point can a man like Ma Tzu come to live in the marketplace, because he knows that his mirror is not any conceptualization, it is now his experience. He knows that everything is reflected. People come and go, riches come and go, the poor become rich, the rich become poor; things go on happening, but your mirror simply mirrors.

Ma Tzu has come to the very root of the problem. If you can understand him, then, in a single moment, instantaneously, the awakening can happen to you too.

At another time, Ma Tzu said, "Every dharma is the dharma of the mind, and every name is a name of the mind. All beings are born of the mind, and so mind is the foundation of all beings.

"As an example: the shadow of the moon reflected on the water has many shapes, but the real moon is not like that. Likewise there are various rivers, but the nature of the water is the same. Although there are myriad activities, there is no discrimination in the emptiness."

Ma Tzu uses the word 'mind', but you have to understand that his 'mind' means 'empty mind', a mind which is emptiness. If the mirror is already full of reflections, it cannot reflect you. The mirror is no more a mirror, it has become a film of a camera. You can take one image on the film, and the film is finished, because that image remains on the film. The film is very much identified with the image; the film does not function like the mirror.

Empty mind is the origin of all—all the dharmas, every name, all beings. Empty mind is the foundation of all things. Realizing that empty mind is the foundation of all things; all that you have to do is to throw away all the furniture that you have gathered in your mind. It is all junk. It is destroying your precious spaciousness.

Have you ever thought about the word 'room'? Do you know that the word 'room' means spaciousness, roominess? When a room is full of furniture and all kinds of things, photographs, and flowers, its roominess is covered. It is less roomy, less spacious than its reality. If you remove everything from the room, it can be described as an empty room; but that is really repeating the word. 'Room' simply means emptiness, spaciousness.

That's why Ma Tzu does not use the two words together: 'empty' and 'mind'.

To him 'mind' itself means 'emptiness', it is another name for 'emptiness'. And out of this emptiness everything arises.

It was thought to be a very mysterious idea, unbelievable, but now science has to concede that the philosophers and the objective scientists have been wrong, and the mystics have been right. Now they can see...and you can see it in everyday life. Have you ever taken a seed and cut it into two? Do you find any roses inside it? Or do you find any kind of foliage? You find simply nothingness.

But the same seed, given the right opportunity and climate, the right soil and a loving gardener, will start sprouting as the spring comes. Those green leaves that come in the beginning...because you are so much accustomed to seeing all this, you don't see the mystery of it. From where are those two leaves coming? You have looked into the seed, there were no leaves in it, no roses in it. And now there is a great foliage of thousands of leaves and hundreds of flowers. From where? From nowhere; from the emptiness of existence they arise.

And then one day the flowers disappear, the leaves fall away, the tree disappears. Where? Where has it all gone? Again to rest, into emptiness.

Now science is agreeing that even great stars...and their greatness is really shocking even to think of. We think of them as small stars, but they are not small. They are very far away, that is why they look small. Our own sun is a star. It is six hundred times bigger than our earth, and it is considered to be, in the universe of stars, a mediocre star, a middle-class fellow—because there are stars thousands of times bigger than this.

And every day hundreds of stars are dying—but where do they disappear to? And hundreds of stars are born, so the balance remains. From where?

Just within these last twenty years they have found things that make the whole of science such a mystery. They found black holes first; they found that there are black holes in the sky, and what they are exactly nobody knows. But if any star comes close to a black hole—the black hole has a gravity thousands of times greater than the earth—the star simply goes into the black hole and disappears. Just a moment before it was there in its immense glory, and just a moment afterwards there is just nothing but darkness. The star has gone back to rest, into emptiness.

After the black hole, it was natural and inevitable to find white holes—because if the black hole takes stars into emptiness, there must be white holes from where new stars are born. And now they are agreed on the fact that there are white holes, which go on throwing out new stars.

My own feeling is that perhaps it is the same hole—on one side black, on the other side white. So you jump through the door; from one side you are dead, from another side you come out smiling. This is my own feeling, I am not saying that it is scientific. I don't care about science or anything, but this seems to be more possible, rather than black holes in one place, and white holes far away from them... that does not look right. They should be close enough, so as the old star becomes empty, from the white door it gains a new incarnation, and comes back again.

But as far as emptiness is concerned, nothing makes any mark on it. It remains utterly empty.

"Different things go through the different ways, but the liberated wisdom is one. All are based on one empty mind.

"Every dharma is based on the dharma of Buddha. Each dharma is instantly the dharma of realization, and the dharma of realization is, things being as they really are."

To see things as they really are, you have to be absolutely empty —only a mirror. Your mirror should be clean, without any dust, without any thought, without any prejudice, without any religion. Just a pure reflective mirror, and you can see things as they are. And seeing things as they are, life becomes a festival, a celebration, a dance. The whole existence is dancing, rejoicing; it is drunk completely with blissfulness, except for man—who is unnecessarily keeping himself filled with junk in his mind, and preventing his mirror from reflecting the reality of existence.

"All that come and go and have a rest, or sit and lie down, are the

mysterious work, and they don't need a process of time. The scriptures also say: 'All around everywhere, instantaneously there are buddhas.'"

I don't care about scriptures, but I can see everywhere, all around, there are buddhas. It is not a quotation from any scripture, I can see it with my own eyes. You may not be aware, that does not matter. A man of clarity will be able to see your reality. And the function of the master is to point again and again to your reality. It is a kind of harassment to go on hitting on your head, the way a nail is hit into the wall, so that finally you scream, and you say, "Yes, I am a buddha!"

Unless you scream, and say "I am a buddha!" the master is going to hammer the nail into your head. But most people, just seeing the hammer, immediately realize, "What is the point of unnecessary suffering? Why not be a buddha?"

That's how I became a buddha. Seeing that other fellows are becoming buddhas instantaneously, why should I waste time? And the day I recognized that there is no need of any effort, that I am a born buddha—since that time, not for a single moment has any doubt arisen. I have tried myself to doubt the fact—"Just think twice, you may not be a buddha"—but I have been a failure. That instantaneous experience of buddhahood has gone so deep that now no doubt arises. On the contrary, every day I go on becoming more and more beyond doubt, beyond any question. And strangely enough, since the day I became aware of my buddhahood, all misery has disappeared, all suffering has disappeared. I don't have any tensions. I don't think about tomorrow.

Just after harassing you a little, I will go to sleep, not even thinking that there is going to be another sunrise. In the morning, when Nirvano wakes me, I say, "My God, again? The whole day...and in the evening the same harassment of poor buddhas."

An unnecessary effort, if you understand; just recognize it yourself—don't let me harass you!

Ma Tzu continued, "Cultivation is of no use for the attainment of Tao."

Call it Tao, or the buddha, or the dharma—it is the same. *Cultivation is of no use...* Don't try to cultivate, just be! For one day

162

try it at least, not cultivating; just for twenty-four hours give me a chance! Be a buddha whatever happens. And I don't think you will come back again to be a non-buddha. Twenty-four hours, if you can maintain your buddhahood whatever happens... Your wife escapes, don't be worried! A buddha does not get worried. At the most you can do one thing, which is proper; go to the post office and report that your wife has escaped. Don't go to the police station, because the police station is a dangerous place—they may bring your wife back! And the one she has gone with is your best friend.

Just relax and enjoy it, "How grateful I am to the universe. It happens to very few, rare individuals!" The wife, and escaping? Most wives cling so hard that they take all juice out of you. You are just moving without any juice. To be a buddha it is perfectly good, it is absolutely necessary, that somebody should escape with your wife.

One of my friends, who presented me with my first car, asked me after one year, "Do you get angry sometimes? Because I have never seen a driver who will not get angry on the Indian roads."

I said, "Let it be on record, because no buddha before has ever driven a car. I simply see the things as they are: the road is rotten, and it is going to be more rotten tomorrow."

In forty years of independence it has been going down and down and down. Nobody seems to be interested that roads have to be repaired. Nobody follows the traffic laws because it is a free country! You are blessed if you come back home alive. You can just go in Poona and see the traffic—that's why I lie down in my room. Why unnecessarily get into trouble?

But I told my friend that I don't get angry—what is the point? Getting angry at the road? I don't get angry with the strange traffic that goes on around. It is a free country, everybody is free to follow his own ideas. So somebody follows to the left, somebody follows to the right, and there are people who follow in the middle.

But it's not much of a problem. In countries where traffic rules are very strict, the rate of accidents is greater than in India—that is a miracle. It has been found that in America, where traffic rules are very strict and you cannot drive more that fifty-five miles per hour, more people die in accidents than in India, where you can drive anywhere you like, and where on the road it is not just the twentieth century, but all the centuries together: a bullock cart is going, somebody is driving a camel cart, an elephant is moving; and dogs have freedom in India as they have nowhere else in the world, and children are playing football in the road.

Still, one goes to the office, one comes back alive. I don't go anywhere, but every morning I am surprised, "My God, again!"

But there is no anger, there is no complaint, there is no grudge. I will enjoy one day more. There must be one morning that I will not wake up; I will enjoy that too. I simply enjoy the idea that you are all trying to wake me up, and I simply don't wake up! The same game that I have been trying so long: trying to wake you up, and nobody is waking. One day, you will be in the same position.

Ma Tzu says, *"The only thing that one can do is to be free of defilement. When one's mind is stained with thoughts of life and death, or deliberate action, that is defilement."*

You can see, his use of 'mind' is equivalent to 'no-mind'. When the mind becomes defiled *with thoughts of life and death, or deliberate action, that is defilement.* Then the mind is full of imagination, of thoughts, of emotions, of sentiments, of past memories, of future utopias. And the mirror is completely lost in layers of dust. You don't have to cultivate anything, you have just to drop all this dust that has gathered on your mirror.

The grasping of the truth is not something special, it *is the function of everyday-mindedness.*

Just keep your mind undefiled, and the whole world looks so clean, so pure, so immensely beautiful, that you cannot but be grateful.

"Everyday-mindedness is free from intentional action, free from concepts of right and wrong, taking and giving, the finite or the infinite.... All our daily activities—walking, standing, sitting, lying down—all response to situations, our dealings with circumstances as they arise: all this is Tao."

Ma Tzu is against, just as I am against, those who escape from the world, renounce the world. Those people are not saints, they have simply chickened out! They could not encounter the existence with a right, clean mirror. They escaped, being afraid that they would be defiled by others. Nobody can defile you. It is up to you; if you allow dust to gather on your mirror, there will be defilement. If you don't allow dust...

There is a Zen story:

A Zen master sent his chief disciple to a caravanserai for his last examination. The disciple said, "What kind of examination is this? What am I to do in that caravanserai?"

He said, "You just go and watch whatever is happening there, and bring the news to me. That is going to decide whether you are going to be my successor or not."

He went to the caravanserai, he watched everything. It was a question of tremendous importance, and what he brought made him the successor.

He brought this: "I saw that the owner of the caravanserai cleans the mirror in the evening—each evening—and again in the morning he cleans the mirror. So I asked him, 'You cleaned it just a few hours ago, why are you cleaning it again?' The owner said, 'The dust goes on gathering every moment, so clean the mirror whenever you have time. You will always find some dust which has gathered.'

"And I have come to the conclusion that you were right to send me to the caravanserai. This is actually the case with the mind—clean it every moment, because every moment, just by its nature, dust goes on gathering."

If you can avoid defilement, there is no need of any cultivation; you will realize the ultimate truth, the Tao.

A Zen haiku:

Entering the forest,
he moves not the grass.
Entering the water,
he makes not a ripple.

He is talking about the full moon. A full moon entering into the forest moves not even the grass. So silent...its movement is so graceful that not even the grass is disturbed. Entering the water as a reflection, he makes not a ripple.

And that is the state of the awakened man, the buddha. Even entering into the marketplace he makes no ripples. Wherever he is, he is just an undefiled mirror. Nothing disturbs it, nothing becomes attached to it—like a cloud. Everything comes and goes, and the mirror remains all the time empty. If you can be empty, you are enlightened. Such a simple and obvious phenomenon, it does not need any cultivation.

Now, the question that has created in Maneesha a migraine, so that Anando has to represent her. She has asked:

Our Beloved Master,
A situation that occurred last night was such a vivid illustration for me of how You are—as we have heard of Ma Tzu—a living teaching master of Zen, a man of Tao.
When the horse came trotting into the hall, anyone in Your place who was anything less than enlightened would have been disconcerted to find that the attention had moved from them. They may have felt distracted, thrown off center; afraid of looking foolish because they could not see what the cause of the laughter was.
You simply stopped talking and allowed events to take a new course. You looked so vulnerable, so innocent and unknowing, in those moments. Your immense power and extraordinary fragility, Your absolute presence and Your utter absence were so apparent.
This is not really a question; I just wanted an excuse to make sure the incident did not go unrecorded.

This question – which is not a question – has created in poor Maneesha a migraine. She must have felt, how is she going to read it to me? But she is perfectly right, and she need not be worried that just for the record she has asked a question which is not a question.

In Maneesha I have found a better recorder than Ramakrishna had in Vivekananda, or even Socrates had in Plato. She records everything perfectly well, that's why she has become shy—it is not a migraine. Tomorrow she will be here again.

There is no need to be afraid, you can ask me anything. You can give any record of events. I enjoyed last night's episode. It is not that I was annoyed, I was enjoying it so tremendously because it was such an unexpected phenomenon. I thought perhaps Kalki, the white horse, had come; because his time is close—just twelve years more. By the end of this century Kalki is going to come. So I thought if he has come here it is a really great moment, and here there will be no need for him to make any judgments because all are sinners!

And he came a little early, because inside him was great Avirbhava, and Avirbhava's associate, Anando, and naturally inside that horse you cannot remain long. One must be feeling suffocated. So they came a little early. It was Anando who was pulling Avirbhava back, "This is not time!"—but Avirbhava jumped in.

It would have been a great accident if the horse had fallen in two. That would have been absolutely against the tradition, and somebody would have put a case against me, that their religious feelings are hurt—Kalki breaking down in the middle.

But they both managed perfectly well.

Now, soon I will be sending Avirbhava to find... There are coats available for lions, for tigers, for elephants. You just have to be a little patient, and don't run off the track, don't enter the crowd. In most of the circuses where you see the lions roaring, you just watch a little closely; so many lions are not available....

I have heard about one case:

A man asked for employment in a circus. The manager said, "It is a very dangerous job. One lion has died, so you will have to enter into his skin and behave like a lion; and you will be surrounded by real lions. It is a dangerous job, I make you aware from the very beginning."

He was so desperate that he accepted the job; the salary was good. But as he entered into the skin of the lion, and was led into the cage, he freaked out. There was another lion just roaring, so he started shouting, "Help me!"

The whole crowd that had gathered to see had never seen such a scene, that a lion is asking for help, in perfect English! And the other lion said to him, "You idiot! Don't freak out, otherwise we both will lose our jobs."

He used to be the headmaster, and this other fellow used to be the teacher in the school; and they had both lost their jobs.

You can find, Avirbhava, good lions, tigers, elephants, crocodiles, and all kinds of weirdos. Your Museum of Gods has to become one of the richest museums in the world. In fact there is no comparison anywhere; nobody has bothered to collect information about ancient gods, modern gods.

Today you heard the noise on the street—it is for the elephant god. It is such a humiliation of man, that he has been forced to worship all kinds of animals. Rather than helping him to become a buddha, they are forcing him to become lower than animals. Our effort is to expose all those religions who have exploited man, insulted man, humiliated mankind.

Maneesha, your recording is perfectly good. Next time when you feel the migraine, still come. When people do two minutes' gibberish, throw away your migraine—somebody will catch it! Just throw it far away. Everybody is trying it a double way: he is throwing his things out, and moving his hands to protect himself, because others are also throwing out all kinds of bullshit. One has to protect oneself—just exchanging your bullshit will not help.

It is time for Sardar Gurudayal Singh.

"Oh, it is such a sad story," sobs Jablonski into his beer at the Fried Fisherman pub.

"What is the matter?" asks his pal, Klopski.

"It is my kid, Albert," says Jablonski. "For years, day after day, little Albert and his dog went to school together, until, sadly, the day came when they had to part."

"What happened?" exclaims Klopski.

"Well," says Jablonski, "the dog graduated!"

It is that fateful night, when Jesus has been nailed to the cross. He has been up there for about five hours, when he looks down with surprise.

"No! No!" he shouts. "Get away, get away!"

But it does no good.

Then he starts really freaking out. He screams again, *"Go away!"*

But it does not work.

The cross starts shaking and leaning, and, as it falls over, Jesus cries, "Fucking beavers!"

Doctor Skinbag's patients keep calling him in the middle of the night. So, one weekend, he has a talk with his wife, Sally.

"Listen," says Skinbag, "I am completely worn out. I need some peace and quiet. If any of my patients call, just tell them that I am out of town at a medical meeting."

That night, the phone rings at two o'clock. Sally Skinbag answers it, and tells the caller that Doctor Skinbag is out of town.

"But, Mrs. Skinbag, my grandad is coughing and spluttering, and I don't know what to do!" says Mrs. Klutz, the caller.

"Just a minute," says Sally, covering the phone, and asking Doctor Skinbag what to tell Mrs. Klutz.

"Tell her to put the old guy into his iron lung," says Skinbag.

"Mrs. Klutz," says Sally, into the phone, "put your grandad into the iron lung."

"Oh, thank you, Mrs. Skinbag," replies Mrs. Klutz, "but for how long?"

"Just a minute," says Sally, as she turns to Skinbag again.

"Tell her for half an hour," says Skinbag.

"Put him in for half an hour," repeats Sally into the phone.

"Oh, thank you," replies Mrs. Klutz. "But I just have one more question for you. Is that guy you are in bed with also a doctor?"

Old lady Muffet's proudest possession is a beautiful white Persian cat named Conrad. But Grandma Muffet notices that Conrad has been missing for two days. When she goes to the freezer that night for dinner, she nearly dies of shock. There is Conrad, sitting on a plate, frozen solid.

Grandma frantically calls her vet, Doctor Ratso, and asks what she should do.

"There is still a chance to save the poor animal," says Dr. Ratso. "Give it two teaspoons of gasoline."

With trembling hands, Grandma Muffet cracks open Conrad's frozen lips, and carefully spoons in the doctor's strange prescription.

The seconds tick by, and nothing happens.

Grandma is just about to give up hope, when suddenly the cat's eyes pop open, it lets out an ear-piercing scream, and flies across the room at three hundred miles an hour.

It runs over all the furniture, scratches up and down the walls, and dashes across the ceiling. The cat streaks around the apartment like a furious hurricane, then suddenly stops dead in its tracks—not moving a muscle.

Quickly, Grandma phones Dr. Ratso again.

"What do you think happened?" she cries.

"Simple," replies Ratso. "He just ran out of gas!"

Nivedano...

Nivedano…

Be silent.
Close your eyes.
Feel your body to be frozen.
Look inwards with absolute urgency,
as if this is the moment of life and death.
Without a total urgency, you cannot reach
to the innermost center of your being.
Remember, there may be no other time;
this may be the last moment.
Deeper and deeper, without any fear,
move into the center like an arrow.
It is your own life-source,
and it is also the life-source of the whole universe.
This is the ultimate home—
the buddha, the empty mirror of Ma Tzu.
Just be a witness, a clean mirror reflecting everything
without any judgment.
To make it more clear, Nivedano…

Relax,
and see that your body is not you,
your mind is not you,
you are just a witness.
This witness I have called the mirror.
This is your eternity,
this is your ultimate nature of buddhahood.
Once you have tasted it,
once you have walked the path to the life stream,
you will never be the same again.
Finally you have to awaken as a perfect buddha.
To the eyes of a buddha,
the whole existence becomes enlightened.
The green of the trees become greener,
the fragrance of the roses takes a new nuance,
the full moon in the night reflects in your mirror
without creating any ripples.
The whole of life becomes a festival,
a ceremony, a rejoicing.
This evening and this silence
make it a beautiful experience.
You are all dissolved
into one oceanic consciousness;
separation is forgotten, oneness is remembered.
Carry this ecstasy, this drunkenness,
twenty-four hours around the clock.
Except this there is no other religion.
Nivedano...

Now come back,
but come back as a buddha,
without any hesitation,
silently and peacefully,
with the grace and beauty of a buddha.
Just recollect the experience.
You have to live it moment to moment,
day and night,
speaking or in silence,
working or resting;
but the buddha remains
a constant undercurrent in you.
Then you don't need any morality,
you don't need any religion,
you don't need anything.
You have got the very key—
the master key—
that opens the doors
of all the mysteries of existence.

Okay, Maneesha, care of Anando?
Yes, Beloved Master.
Can we celebrate the ten thousand buddhas?
Yes, Beloved Master.

moon-face

Our Beloved Master,
Ma Tzu was one day teaching a monk. He drew a circle on the ground and said, "If you enter it, I will strike you; if you do not enter it, I will strike you!"
The monk entered it slightly, and Ma Tzu struck him.
The monk said, "The master could not strike me!"
Ma Tzu went off leaning on his staff.

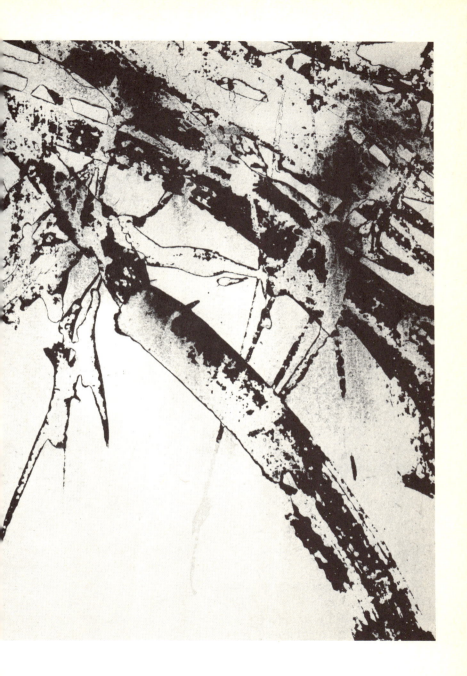

On another occasion, Ho Pang said to Ma Tzu, "Water has no bones, but it easily holds up a ship of a thousand tons; how is this?"
Ma Tzu said, "There's no water here, and no ship—what am I supposed to explain?"

One day, Impō was pushing a cart, and Ma Tzu had his legs stretched out across the path. Impō said, "Please, master, pull in your legs!"
"What has been stretched out," said Ma Tzu, "cannot be retracted!"
"What goes forward cannot go backwards!" said Impō and pushed the cart on.
Ma Tzu's legs were cut and bruised. When they went back, Ma Tzu entered the hall, and said, lifting up an axe, "Come here, the monk who hurt my legs a while ago!" Impō came out and stood before Ma Tzu and bent his neck to receive the strike.
Ma Tzu put down the axe.

Ma Tzu never lost an opportunity to make a point, usually in an enigmatic way. Even during his last illness he made his well-known response to someone who inquired about his health. He said, "Sun-faced buddhas, moon-faced buddhas."
One day, Ma Tzu climbed Mount Sekimon, the mountain close to his temple at Chiang-si. In the forest he did kinhin, or walking meditation, for a time. Then, seeing a flat place in the valley below, Ma Tzu said to the disciple who had come with him, "Next month, my carcass must be returned to the earth here." At that, he made his way back to the temple.
On the fourth day of the next month, after bathing, he quietly sat down with crossed legs and passed away.
Ma Tzu had lived at Chiang-si for fifty years and died at the age of eighty.

maneesha, I have asked you to throw your migraine, and you did it. But you did it too close by, on poor Anando. She is my only link with the world. She is my news media, my television, my radio, my newspapers. I don't read anything, I don't hear anything, I don't see anything on the television. And because we were talking about the empty heart, your throwing was perfectly good—but it reached into the wrong place, in poor Anando. It had to reach her head, but it has reached into her heart.

Her empty heart has received your migraine. Now, there is no such sickness in the whole world, and Doctor Indivar will be in immense difficulty to pull out the migraine from the heart. It is perfectly okay to have the mirror in the empty heart, but it is not right to have a migraine. There exists no medicine for it; Doctor Indivar will have to invent something—and I need her back urgently, because every morning, every evening she is my only contact with the world.

So as far as Anando is concerned, it is Indivar's priority. And just because she received the migraine with the open heart, she has earned great virtue. The next series that begins tomorrow will be dedicated to her. She did perfectly well in keeping the heart open, even when you were throwing your migraine away. Most people will close their windows and doors in such situations. But she is a great disciple, and she understands intelligently what it means to have an open heart, to live in insecurity, to live without any safety, to be homeless.

But Anando—you must be hearing me from your room—remember, no buddha has said, "Keep your heart open when somebody is throwing a migraine." You have done a miracle. There is an automatic system—if somebody is throwing dust at you, your eyes will close without any effort, on their own. And if somebody is throwing a migraine, naturally the heart will close. It will not receive it. But you dared to keep your heart open. You showed great courage. I can rely on you, that whatever happens you will keep your heart open. It may be painful, it may create anxiety, but that is only the beginning part.

Gautam Buddha is reported to have said, "What is bitter in the beginning is sweet in the end, and what is sweet in the beginning is bitter at the end." It is an immense statement about all those who are the people of the path.

The story Maneesha has brought:
Ma Tzu was one day teaching a monk. He drew a circle on the ground and said, "If you enter it, I will strike you; if you do not enter it, I will strike you!"

This is something very special in Zen. In different ways masters have used that device. If you say something, I will strike you; if you don't say something, I will strike you. In any case you will get the hit. The same is the situation here.

Ma Tzu says, *"If you enter this circle, I will strike you; if you do not enter it, I will strike you all the same!" The monk entered it slightly, and Ma Tzu struck him.*

What is the point of this strange anecdote?

The monk said, "The master could not strike me!" Ma Tzu went off leaning on his staff, not even bothering to answer the disciple.

In any devices that are similar, in either case you will get the hit. It simply means that the hit is meant to awaken you. What you do is not relevant—whether you enter the circle or stay out of it, it does not matter, I am going to hit you! This simply means that whatever you do is not important; what is important is your awakening. The hit is to wake you up. If the disciple can understand what is being asked, he will be enlightened. The master is asking him to be enlightened, so that he does not need to be hit.

But the disciple missed. He said to the master, *"The master could not strike me!" Ma Tzu went off leaning on his staff,* leaving the student behind to meditate over what has happened. Ma Tzu used all kinds of devices spontaneously, but there is always a hidden secret. In the strangest incidents the awakened person will immediately see the hidden secret.

On another occasion, Ho Pang said to Ma Tzu, "Water has no bones, but it easily holds up a ship of a thousand tons; how is this?"

Ma Tzu said, "There's no water here, and no ship—what am I supposed to explain?"

He is saying, "Don't bring intellectual, philosophical questions to me. I am here only to bring existential experience to you."

I am reminded of a small story.

In a court there were two friends who were known in the whole city to be great friends, always together, but finally they were caught fighting and brought to the court by the police. And the magistrate asked, "What is the problem that created the fight?"

They both looked at each other and said, "You say it."

The other said, "Please, you say it."

The magistrate said, "Anybody can say it but just say it."

They said, "We are very embarrassed. We are ready to take any punishment if you allow us not to say it."

The magistrate said, "This is strange. I cannot punish you unless I know the crime. What was the reason for your fighting and creating chaos in the crowd?"

Finally they had to say it. One of them said, "Please forgive us. It is very philosophical, airy, abstract. We were sitting on the river bank and my friend told me that he was going to purchase a buffalo.

"I said, 'I have no objection. Just remember that I am going to purchase a big farm. Your buffalo should never enter into my farm. I am a very strict person.'

"The other man said, 'Your farm? Nobody can stop my buffalo. And I will see how you can stop my buffalo. You are my friend, you should welcome my buffalo; on the contrary you are going to stop it. What kind of friendship is this?'

"I said, 'Friendship does not come into it. Business is business.'

"The man who was going to purchase a buffalo, he said, 'Okay, I will see. Purchase the farm.' And I made a square on the sand with my finger and said, 'This is my farm. Where is your buffalo?'

"The other man with his finger entered into my field and said, 'This is my buffalo. Let us see what you can do.' That's how the whole thing started."

The magistrate said, "But where is the farm and where is the buffalo?"

They said, "That is the problem that we were embarrassed to tell you; it is a very philosophical thing. Nothing is there—no buffalo, no farm, just hot air. But we forgot completely that we were fighting about imaginary things."

You can laugh at it, but do you think…? People have been fighting over the existence of God—is it in any way different from the buffalo? People have been fighting over how many hells there are. The Hindus believe in one hell; the Jainas believe in three hells, because according to them one hell is not justified for all kinds of criminals. Somebody has just stolen a chicken, and somebody has killed a man. You cannot put both the men in the same hell. That will be unjustified. So they have three hells, according to your sin.

But Gautam Buddha had seven. He says that in three you cannot categorize all the crimes; at least seven are needed. But you will be surprised, another philosopher, contemporary to Mahavira and Gautam Buddha, Ajit Keshkambal, had seventy-seven. He said, "Unless you have that number of hells, it will be very difficult to categorize."

Now, nobody knows where this hell is...and they were fighting tooth and nail! And for centuries their philosophers have been fighting, trying to explain their position. For example Hindus have explained that the hell is one, but we can make divisions in the hell. You can make as many divisions as you want in one hell, what is the need of seventy-seven hells? Just make seventy-seven divisions in one hell. But you don't think that these people are idiots; these are great philosophers. But their problems about God... Nobody has met God, it is purely a concept.

And there are religions who don't believe in God. Jainism has no God, Buddhism has no God, Taoism has no God. God is not an essential phenomenon for any religion to exist. And then there are different descriptions of God. The Old Testament says that God is a very angry God, very jealous and very temperamental—don't annoy him. And God himself is reported to have said in the Old Testament, "I am a very jealous God. And remember it, I am your father, not your uncle. Don't expect any nice things from me."

And Jesus says, "God is love."

Hindus say, "God is pure justice"—because love cannot be just; it may love someone and forgive him, it may not love someone, or even dislike someone and punish him unnecessarily for sins that he has not committed. Love is not reliable. God has to be just, a magistrate with no likings, no dislikings.

This anecdote, when Ma Tzu says, *There's no water here, and no ship—what am I supposed to explain?* has all these implications. Then don't get engaged in abstract concepts—those arguments and philosophical discussions are unending, and nobody has come to any conclusion.

The Christian God has a small family: the only begotten son, Jesus Christ, and the Holy Ghost—a strange family with no woman in it, unless this Holy Ghost is capable of functioning as a woman also. But certainly the Holy Ghost is not a woman because he is responsible for making Mary the virgin pregnant with Jesus Christ. And on the other hand, the Christians say that the Holy Ghost and God are one. So why separate them just for the sake of saving God from corrupting and raping an innocent girl? If they are one, then why not say, "God impregnated Mary"; why not make it straightforward? Why should God go via the Holy Ghost? Sometimes I think the Holy Ghost must be God's sexual machinery. So he *is* one, yet he remains outside and the Holy Ghost does the whole work.

Hindus say that their God has three faces, three heads on one body. Now nobody has seen... Perhaps in a circus you may see a distorted child, a freak who has three heads or four hands. But why should God have three heads? The reason given by the Hindu theologians is so that he can see in three directions. If man can manage with one head...perhaps God's neck is fixed, he cannot move this way or that way. Obviously he will need three pairs of glasses. And the weight of three heads on a body which looks exactly like a man's—it will be too much. He will not be able to stand up, and lying down also will be very difficult. Just think, how will he manage his three heads on one pillow?—unless those three heads are only attached and you can unscrew them, and put them off for the night and go to sleep.

But I don't think that such surgery has developed even today. And God has been there for eternity, and no scripture describes any surgeon who takes care of God's heads. The screws must have got rusted. And from where can he get a screwdriver? And you can be sure that three heads may not agree on any point, they will all have their opinions. I don't think that God can move even a single inch because the other two heads will not be ready. So he will remain fixed in one position.

But strange ideas... Hindus also have the idea that God has one thousand hands. Now, three heads and one thousand hands, who are you kidding? Even if you just visualize him, you will become afraid.

He will look like an octopus, or something like it.

Buddhism and Jainism, seeing the difficulty of how to visualize God, simply dropped the idea; they don't have any God and they are perfectly living religions.

Ma Tzu is saying that he is not interested in anything that is not existential. That is Zen's special contribution to human consciousness. Don't be bothered about imaginary conceptual philosophical things, just pin down everything to existence.

> One day, Impō was pushing a cart, and Ma Tzu had his legs stretched out across the path. Impō said, "Please, master, pull in your legs!"
> "What has been stretched out," said Ma Tzu, "cannot be retracted!"
> "What goes forward cannot go backwards!" said Impō and pushed the cart on.
> Ma Tzu's legs were cut and bruised. When they went back, Ma Tzu entered the hall, and said, lifting up an axe, "Come here, the monk who hurt my legs a while ago!" Impō came out and stood before Ma Tzu and bent his neck to receive the strike.
> Ma Tzu put down the axe.

Reading such anecdotes, one feels it is a very strange religion. It is not. Everything that is happening in these anecdotes has something essential, so that you can become aware of it.

First, Ma Tzu said, "What has been stretched out, cannot be retracted!"

A father was telling to his son, "Everything is possible in the world"—he was quoting Alexander the Great.

The child said, "I don't accept the idea, and I will show you why." He went into the bathroom and brought the toothpaste and said, "I will bring the toothpaste out of the tube, and you put it back. You say nothing is impossible. This is impossible. I have tried."

Ma Tzu is saying, "What has been stretched out, cannot be retracted!" In other words, he is saying that what has become exposed cannot become a secret again; what has come into the open cannot go back into the hidden. He is simply making a point that there are situations where you cannot go back.

When Henry Ford made his first car, it had no reverse gear. It could not move backwards, it could go only forwards. He had not thought about it, but it was a very difficult task. If you have moved just a few yards away from your garage, you have to now go around the whole city to come back to your garage. He added the possibility of backing the car later on.

A story is told that when Henry Ford died there was a great encounter between him and God. God said, "You are a great inventor and a man of great intelligence. Do you approve of my existence?"

Henry Ford said, "No, sir. Your existence is the worst possible, because you cannot go back in time, just forward. This is stupid. I had committed this stupidity myself, but it is not expected from you. Somebody wants to visit his childhood again—there should be some possibility to go back in time, or to go forward in time if somebody wants to know in advance what kind of old age, what kind of death is going to happen, and when. You have left man stuck in the middle; he can neither go back, nor can he go forward. He has no freedom of movement in time. I have great complaints, but this is my most basic complaint to you."

Ma Tzu is saying that if you have become a young man, you cannot become a child again. If you have become old, you cannot become a young person again. If you are dead, you cannot open your eyes and ask for a tea. He used every situation; and he used this situation to see whether the disciple is courageous enough to pull the cart over the legs of the master. Impō proved worthy.

"What goes forward cannot go backwards!" said Impō and pushed the cart on.

Ma Tzu's legs were cut and bruised. When they went back, Ma Tzu entered the hall, and said, lifting up an axe, "Come here, the monk who hurt my legs a while ago!" Impō came out and stood before Ma Tzu and bent his neck to receive the strike.

This is courage and this is trust. It was not in any way insulting to Ma Tzu. By pushing the cart forward he was not in any way humiliating Ma Tzu, he was simply sticking to his own opinion. If Ma Tzu is sticking to his opinion—and Ma Tzu's whole work was to give independence to the disciples... They should not take anything for granted from anybody else; they should decide themselves their lives, their actions, their gestures. Certainly he was following Ma Tzu when he pushed the cart over his legs.

Ma Tzu had one thousand monks in his monastery. He went to the hall for the assembly meeting. He had no idea who the monk was that had pushed the cart over his legs.

He simply said, lifting an axe, *"Come here, the monk who hurt my legs a while ago!" Impō came out* immediately *and stood before Ma Tzu and bent his neck to receive the strike.*

He did not hide. He could have, because there were one thousand monks and it would have been very difficult to decide who was the person. But he came out, and if the master wants to cut his head, he is ready. He has come to the master to have a resurrection, to be enlightened, to go beyond death. If this is the way the master chooses, it is perfectly okay.

Seeing this humbleness and this trust, *Ma Tzu put down the axe.*

Ma Tzu never lost an opportunity to make a point, usually in an enigmatic way. Even during his last illness he made his well-known response to someone who inquired about his health. He said, "Sun-faced buddhas, moon-faced buddhas."

It is a famous saying in Zen circles. Whether you are facing the sun, which means life, day, or whether you are facing the moon, the night, which represents death—it does not make any difference to your buddhahood. Whether your buddha is in darkness or in light, it does not matter. Your self-nature remains the same. *"Sun-faced buddhas, moon-faced buddhas."* In a very short aphorism, even at the point when he was going to die, he said, "There is going to be no change. Just the sun is setting and the moon will be rising. As far as I am concerned, I am eternal. Whether the sun is in the sky, or the moon is in the sky, I am always here."

The master knows no death. He knows eternity.

One day, Ma Tzu climbed Mount Sekimon, the mountain close to his temple at Chiang-si. In the forest he did kinhin, or walking meditation.

If you go to Bodhgaya, where Gautam Buddha became enlightened, you will find a temple raised in the memory of his enlightenment. And also, by the side of the temple, there are stones in a long line, and behind the temple is the bodhi tree where he used to sit. His meditation had two positions, sitting and walking. One hour you sit, silently watching your thoughts; then one hour you walk slowly, again watching your thoughts—alternate sitting and walking meditation.

It is a beautiful experience because soon you become aware that whether you are sitting or walking, whether you are awake or asleep, something in you remains constantly aware, the same. It does not become different when you walk, it does not become different when you sit. It does not become different even when you sleep; something like a small candle or light goes on burning in your sleep too. Your awareness has become a twenty-four-hour circle. This is the perfect enlightenment.

This walking meditation in Japanese is called *kinhin*.

Then, seeing a flat place in the valley below, Ma Tzu said to the disciple who had come with him, "Next month, my carcass must be returned to the earth here." At that, he made his way back to the temple.

On the fourth day of the next month, after bathing, he quietly sat down with crossed legs and passed away.

The master lives with awareness and dies with awareness. Even a month before, he was aware that death is coming close; his perceptivity, his clarity of perception, is total. So he showed the disciple where his dead body has to be brought, where his *samadhi*, his grave is going to be. One month before, he told the disciple, and the next month...*on the fourth day...after bathing, he quietly sat down with crossed legs and passed away.*

Death is just a game, moving from one body to another body, or perhaps moving from the body to no body, to the universal oceanic existence.

One night a thief entered into Mulla Nasruddin's house. He saw that Mulla Nasruddin was fast asleep and he collected everything that he felt was valuable. But Mulla was not asleep, he just did not want to interfere in somebody's work. He looked by opening one eye and then rested. As the thief was going out with all the valuables, he followed him. The thief looked back and became very afraid. He said, "Why are you coming with me?"

Mulla said, "Have you forgotten? We are changing our house. You are taking everything, so why leave me here alone? I am coming with you."

The thief said, "Just forgive me. Take all your things, sort them out, because I have brought things from other houses also."

Mulla said, "I don't want to sort it out. Either I come with you, or everything has to be put back in my house."

The thief said, "My God, you seem to be a greater thief than me! And why did you remain silent when I was collecting things?"

Mulla said, "I never interfere in anybody's work."

The thief had to leave everything—with tears in his eyes, because he had stolen many beautiful things from other places. He said, "Such a man I have never seen in my life…and to take you to my house, perhaps you will become the master and I will be the servant. I have my wife…"

Mulla said, "There is no problem, we can share everything. We are partners. Don't miss this opportunity of having a wise man as your partner." But the thief escaped leaving all the things.

As far as any master's death is concerned, he is simply changing his house. There is not even a single ripple of sadness, but on the contrary an immense curiosity about the unknown that is opening its doors. This body he has lived in long enough—seventy years, eighty years—it is time to change. The body has become old; it is becoming more and more non-functional. It is time to have a fresh new body.

The master is not at all disturbed by the fact that he is going to die. He dies with grace and beauty, he dies in silence and peace—just the way he has lived. He lived in silence, in utter beatitude, he dies in tremendous benediction.

Ma Tzu had lived at Chiang-si for fifty years and died at the age of eighty.

A haiku:

Both plains and mountains have been
captured by the snow—
there is nothing left.

A haiku is a special form of poetry which exists only in Japan. It has very few words but it tells much. Its beauty is that it is a condensed philosophy. And what cannot be said in prose, can sometimes be said in poetry.

Both plains and mountains have been captured by the snow—there is nothing left.

He is describing his own being. Everything has been taken away. Even he has disappeared into the vastness of the universe; nothing is left behind. Just as a dewdrop disappears into the ocean, a man of enlightenment disappears into the universal consciousness. Nothing is left behind.

Maneesha has asked:

Our Beloved Master,
During the last few weeks, whenever You have said the words, 'empty', or 'empty heart', or 'empty mirror', it has felt like a trigger, a reminder that does not just tickle my mind but goes right to that space of emptiness in me.

I heard You say recently that one could not "hate" or "love" enlightenment. Is it all right to love the space of emptiness?

No, Maneesha. If you love the space of emptiness, you will never become empty. You will remain aloof. Emptiness will become an object of love, but you will be there, the lover. The whole effort of meditation is that you should disappear. In your disappearance you cannot say, "I love emptiness." In your disappearance there is love. But it is not your love, it is just a universal phenomenon—spontaneous, blossoming in the emptiness, filling the whole emptiness with the fragrance of love and compassion and truth.

But nothing is yours. You are no more. Unless you are no more, emptiness is not emptiness. You have to dissolve into the vastness of existence. You have not to be; then there is emptiness. And in that emptiness many things blossom, many roses and many lotuses. Much love and much compassion and much beauty, much truth; all that is great, all that is majestic, all that is splendorous arises of its own accord. But it is not your possession. In fact you were the barrier. It is because of you that emptiness could not function. Now you are no more; emptiness functions spontaneously, it blossoms into thousands of flowers.

Now it is Sardar Gurudayal Singh's time.

Three little babies are being pushed in trolleys through the supermarket, while their mothers do the shopping.

"Ah God!" gurgles baby Gilbert. "Do you see that? She's buying canned baby food. I hate that stuff!"

"Oh no!" squeaks baby Sally. "Mine is buying spinach. That stuff is the worst!"

"Jesus Christ!" cries baby Boris, seeing his mother and one of her boyfriends at the liquor counter. "You guys don't have anything to complain about. My mother wakes me up at four o'clock in the morning, pushes a cold wet tit into my mouth, and it always tastes of cigarettes and cheap brandy!"

Little Ernie and his mother are walking through the park one day when little Ernie sees a large, pregnant woman walk by.

"Hey, mom!" says Ernie. "How did that lady get such a big belly?"

Ernie's mother becomes a bit flustered.

"Well, dear," she says, "she got that way from eating too much chocolate."

"Really?" says Ernie with surprise.

Later, waiting at the bus stop, Ernie sees the same pregnant woman standing next to him.

"Hey, lady," says Ernie, poking her belly. "I know what you've been doing—and isn't it far out?"

An elephant and a mouse are walking through the jungle, when the mouse falls into a swamp. He is about to drown, but the elephant straddles the swamp and slowly lowers his prick. The mouse grabs onto the huge piece of machinery and the elephant lifts him to safety.

A few weeks later, the mouse and the elephant are walking through the jungle, when the elephant falls into a swamp. Quick as a flash, the mouse runs off and comes back driving a brandnew red

Ferrari sports car. He backs up to the swamp, attaches a rope to the car, throws the other end to the elephant, jumps back into the Ferrari, and slowly pulls the huge elephant out of the swamp.

...Which just goes to show that if you have a red Ferrari, you don't need a big prick.

Nivedano...

Nivedano...

Be silent.

Close your eyes.
Feel your body to be completely frozen.
Now look inwards as deeply as possible.
You have to reach to the very center of your being.
Deeper and deeper…
Your center of being is also
the center of the whole universe.
The deeper you go, the richer you are.
The deeper you go, the more awakened you are.
At the very center of your being
you will find your buddha nature.
The buddha is hidden in everyone,
we just have to go deep down enough.
To make your witness,
your mirror,
your buddha,
more clear to you,
Nivedano…

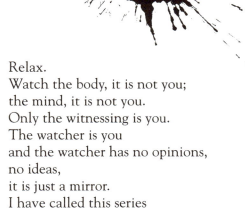

Relax.
Watch the body, it is not you;
the mind, it is not you.
Only the witnessing is you.
The watcher is you
and the watcher has no opinions,
no ideas,
it is just a mirror.
I have called this series

Ma Tzu: The Empty Mirror.
Every meditation is nothing but
the search for the empty mirror,
which reflects but remains utterly empty.
Rejoice in this emptiness
and roses will start appearing.
The experience of buddhahood has to become
your moment-to-moment response around the clock.
Acting or not acting,
working or not working,
speaking or not speaking—
you should remember you are the eternal soul,
the buddha.
As this remembrance deepens in you,
reaches to every fiber and cell of your being,
your life will become a dance,
a poetry, a music, an eternal beauty, a great grace.
Remember this moment,
the space you are in.
This space has to become your very life,
your very death.
This blissfulness has made this evening
a great beauty, a great truth.
Ten thousand buddhas disappearing
into the ocean
like dewdrops.
This is the greatest miracle in the world.
Nivedano…

Come back, but slowly
gathering your experience—
nothing should be left behind—
silently and gracefully.
Sit like a buddha for a few moments,
just watching, just being a mirror.
If you have understood the meaning
of the empty heart
and its becoming just a mirror,
Ma Tzu has not been a failure to you.
These people like Ma Tzu,
or Gautam Buddha, or Lao Tzu,
they don't belong to different centuries.
They are all contemporaries.
The moment you enter into this emptiness,
this mirrorlike reflection,
a silence that knows no boundaries,
you have become a contemporary of Ma Tzu,
of Chuang Tzu, of Gautam Buddha.
These people are beyond time.
They don't belong to any century,
to any country, to any language.
They are all one in the sense
that thousands of rivers
can enter into the ocean
and they all become one.

Okay, Maneesha?
Yes, Beloved Master.
Can we celebrate the gathering of ten thousand
buddhas?
Yes, Beloved Master.

Worldwide Distribution Centers for the Works of Osho Rajneesh

Books by Osho Rajneesh are available in many languages throughout the world. His discourses have been recorded live on audiotape and videotape. There are many recordings of Rajneesh meditation music and celebration music played in His presence, as well as beautiful photographs of Osho Rajneesh. For further information contact one of the distribution centers below:

EUROPE

Belgium
Indu
Rajneesh Meditation Center
Coebergerstr. 40
2018 Antwerpen
Tel.   3/237 2037
Fax   3/216 9871

Denmark
Anwar Distribution
Carl Johansgade 8, 5
2100 Copenhagen
Tel.   01/420 218
Fax   01/147 348

Finland
Unio Mystica Shop
for Meditative Books & Tapes
Albertinkatu 10
P.O. Box 186
00121 Helsinki
Tel.   3580/665 811

Italy
Rajneesh Services Corporation
Via XX Settembre 12
28041 Arona (NO)
Tel.   02/839 2194 (Milan office)
Fax   02/832 3683

Netherlands
De Stad Rajneesh
Cornelis Troostplein 23
1072 JJ Amsterdam
Tel.   020/5732 130
Fax   020/5732 132

Norway
Devananda
Rajneesh Meditation Center
P.O. Box 177 Vinderen
0319 Oslo 3
Tel.   02/491 590

Spain
Distribuciones "El Rebelde"
Estellencs
07192 Mallorca - Baleares
Tel.   71/410 470
Fax   71/719 027

Sweden
Madhur
Rajneesh Meditation Center
Nidalvsgrand 15
12161 Johanneshov / Stockholm
Tel.   08/394 996
Fax   08/184 972

Switzerland
Mingus
Rajneesh Meditation Center
Asylstrasse 11
8032 Zurich
Tel.   01/2522 012

United Kingdom
Purnima Rajneesh Centre
for Meditation
Spring House, Spring Place
London NW5 3BH
Tel.   01/284 1415
Fax   01/267 1848

West Germany
The Rebel
Publishing House GmbH*
Venloer Strasse 5-7
5000 Cologne 1
Tel.   0221/574 0742
Fax   0221/574 0749
Telex 888 1366 rjtrd

* All books available
  AT COST PRICE

Rajneesh Verlag GmbH
Venloer Strasse 5-7
5000 Cologne 1
Tel.   0221/574 0743
Fax   0221/574 0749

Tao Institut
Klenzestrasse 41
8000 Munich 5
Tel.   089/201 6657
Fax   089/201 3056

AMERICA

United States
Chidvilas
P.O. Box 17550
Boulder, CO 80308
Tel.   303/665 6611
Fax   303/665 6612

Ansu Publishing Co., Inc.
19023 SW Eastside Rd
Lake Oswego, OR 97034
Tel.   503/638 5240
Fax   503/638 5101

Nartano
P.O. Box 51171
Levittown,
Puerto Rico 00950-1171
Tel. 809/795 8829

Also available in bookstores
nationwide at Walden Books

Canada
Publications Rajneesh
P.O. Box 331
Outremont H2V 4N1
Tel.   514/276 2680

AUSTRALIA

Rajneesh Meditation & Healing Centre
P.O. Box 1097
160 High Street
Fremantle, WA 6160
Tel.   09/430 4047
Fax   09/384 8557

ASIA

India
Sadhana Foundation*
17 Koregaon Park
Poona 411 001, MS
Tel.   0212/660 963
Fax   0212/664 181

* All books available
  AT COST PRICE

Japan
Eer Rajneesh
Neo-Sannyas Commune
Mimura Building 6-21-34
Kikuna, Kohoku-ku
Yokohama, 222
Tel.   045/434 1981
Fax   045/434 5565

Books by
Osho Rajneesh

ENGLISH LANGUAGE EDITIONS
RAJNEESH PUBLISHERS
Early Discourses and Writings
A Cup of Tea *Letters to Disciples*
From Sex to Superconsciousness
I Am the Gate
The Long and the Short and the All
The Silent Explosion

Meditation
And Now, and Here (Volumes 1&2)
The Book of the Secrets (Volumes 1–5) *Vigyana Bhairava Tantra*
Dimensions Beyond the Known
In Search of the Miraculous (Volume 1)
Meditation: The First and Last Freedom
Meditation: The Art of Ecstasy
The Orange Book *The Meditation Techniques of Bhagwan Shree Rajneesh*
The Perfect Way
The Psychology of the Esoteric

Buddha and Buddhist Masters
The Book of the Books (Volumes 1–4) *The Dhammapada*
The Diamond Sutra *The Vajrachchedika Prajnaparamita Sutra*
The Discipline of Transcendence (Volumes 1–4)
On the Sutra of 42 Chapters
The Heart Sutra *The Prajnaparamita Hridayam Sutra*
The Book of Wisdom (Vols. 1&2) *Atisha's Seven Points of Mind Training*

Indian Mystics:
The Bauls
The Beloved (Volumes 1&2)

Kabir
The Divine Melody
Ecstasy – The Forgotten Language
The Fish in the Sea is Not Thirsty
The Guest
The Path of Love
The Revolution

Krishna
Krishna: The Man and His Philosophy

Jesus and Christian Mystics

Come Follow Me (Volumes 1–4) *The Sayings of Jesus*
I Say Unto You (Volumes 1&2) *The Sayings of Jesus*
The Mustard Seed *The Gospel of Thomas*
Theologia Mystica *The Treatise of St. Dionysius*

Jewish Mystics

The Art of Dying
The True Sage

Sufism

Just Like That
Mojud, The Man with the Inexplicable Life *Excerpts from The Wisdom of the Sands*
The Perfect Master (Volumes 1&2)
The Secret
Sufis: The People of the Path (Volumes 1&2)
Unio Mystica (Volumes 1&2) *The Hadiqa of Hakim Sanai*
Until You Die
The Wisdom of the Sands (Volumes 1&2)

Tantra

Tantra, Spirituality and Sex *Excerpts from The Book of the Secrets*
Tantra: The Supreme Understanding *Tilopa's Song of Mahamudra*
The Tantra Vision (Volumes 1&2) *The Royal Song of Saraha*

Tao

The Empty Boat *The Stories of Chuang Tzu*
The Secret of Secrets (Volumes 1&2) *The Secret of the Golden Flower*
Tao: The Golden Gate (Volumes 1&2)
Tao: The Pathless Path (Volumes 1&2) *The Stories of Lieh Tzu*
Tao: The Three Treasures (Volumes 1–4) *The Tao Te Ching of Lao Tzu*
When the Shoe Fits *The Stories of Chuang Tzu*

The Upanishads

I Am That *Isa Upanishad*
Philosophia Ultima *Mandukya Upanishad*
The Supreme Doctrine *Kenopanishad*
That Art Thou *Sarvasar Upanishad, Kaivalya Upanishad, Adhyatma Upanishad*
The Ultimate Alchemy (Volumes 1&2) *Atma Pooja Upanishad*
Vedanta: Seven Steps to Samadhi *Akshya Upanishad*

Western Mystics

Guida Spirituale *On the Desiderata*
The Hidden Harmony *The Fragments of Heraclitus*
The Messiah (Volumes 1&2) *Commentaries on Kahlil Gibran's The Prophet*
The New Alchemy: To Turn You On *Mabel Collins' Light on the Path*
Philosophia Perennis (Vols. 1&2) *The Golden Verses of Pythagoras*
Zarathustra: A God That Can Dance
  Commentaries on Friedrich Nietzsche's Thus Spoke Zarathustra

Zarathustra: The Laughing Prophet
Commentaries on Friedrich Nietzsche's Thus Spoke Zarathustra

Yoga

Yoga: The Alpha and the Omega (Volumes 1–10) *The Yoga Sutras of Patanjali*
Yoga: The Science of the Soul (Volumes 1–3)
Original title Yoga: The Alpha and the Omega (Volumes 1–3)

Zen and Zen Masters:

Poona 1974-1981

Ah, This!
Ancient Music in the Pines
And the Flowers Showered
Dang Dang Doko Dang
The First Principle
The Grass Grows By Itself
Hsin Hsin Ming: The Book of Nothing *Discourses on the Faith-Mind of Sosan*
Nirvana: The Last Nightmare
No Water, No Moon
Returning to the Source
Roots and Wings
The Search *The Ten Bulls of Zen*
A Sudden Clash of Thunder
The Sun Rises in the Evening
Take it Easy (Volumes 1&2) *Poems of Ikkyu*
This Very Body the Buddha *Hakuin's Song of Meditation*
Walking in Zen, Sitting in Zen
The White Lotus *The Sayings of Bodhidharma*
Zen: The Path of Paradox (Volumes 1–3)
Zen: The Special Transmission

The Mystery School 1986-present

Bodhidharma The Greatest Zen Master
Commentaries on the Teachings of the Messenger of Zen from India to China
The Great Zen Master Ta Hui
Reflections on the Transformation of an Intellectual to Enlightenment
THE WORLD OF ZEN *A boxed set of 5 volumes, containing:* *
    Live Zen
    This. This. A Thousand Times This.
    Zen: The Quantum Leap from Mind to No-Mind
    Zen: The Solitary Bird, Cuckoo of the Forest
    Zen: The Diamond Thunderbolt
ZEN: ALL THE COLORS OF THE RAINBOW *A boxed set of 5 volumes, containing:* *
    The Miracle
    Turning In
    The Original Man
    The Language of Existence
    The Buddha: The Emptiness of the Heart

OSHO RAJNEESH: THE PRESENT DAY AWAKENED ONE SPEAKS ON THE ANCIENT
  MASTERS OF ZEN *A boxed set of 7 volumes, containing: ⁎*
    Dōgen, the Zen Master: A Search and a Fulfillment
    Ma Tzu: The Empty Mirror
    Hyakujō: The Everest of Zen, with Bashō's Haikus
    Nansen: The Point of Departure
    Jōshū: The Lion's Roar
    Rinzai: Master of the Irrational
    Isan: No Footprints in the Blue Sky
  Each volume is also available individually

Responses to Questions:

Poona 1974-1981
Be Still and Know
The Goose is Out!
My Way: The Way of the White Clouds
Walk Without Feet, Fly Without Wings and Think Without Mind
The Wild Geese and the Water
Zen: Zest, Zip, Zap and Zing

Rajneeshpuram
From Darkness to Light *Answers to the Seekers of the Path*
From the False to the Truth *Answers to the Seekers of the Path*
The Rajneesh Bible (Volumes 1–4)

The World Tour
Light on the Path *Talks in the Himalayas*
The Sword and the Lotus *Talks in the Himalayas*
Socrates Poisoned Again After 25 Centuries *Talks in Greece*
Beyond Psychology *Talks in Uruguay*
The Path of the Mystic *Talks in Uruguay*
The Transmission of the Lamp *Talks in Uruguay*

The Mystery School 1986 – present
Beyond Enlightenment
The Golden Future
The Great Pilgrimage: From Here to Here
The Hidden Splendor
The Invitation
The New Dawn
The Rajneesh Upanishad
The Razor's Edge
The Rebellious Spirit
Sermons in Stones
YAA-HOO! The Mystic Rose
THE MANTRA SERIES:
    Satyam-Shivam-Sundram *Truth-Godliness-Beauty*
    Sat-Chit-Anand *Truth-Consciousness-Bliss*
    Om Mani Padme Hum *The Sound of Silence: The Diamond in the Lotus*

Hari Om Tat Sat *The Divine Sound: That is the Truth*
Om Shantih Shantih Shantih *The Soundless Sound: Peace, Peace, Peace*

Personal Glimpses
Books I Have Loved
Glimpses of a Golden Childhood
Notes of a Madman

Interviews with the World Press
The Last Testament (Volume 1)

Compilations
Beyond the Frontiers of the Mind
Bhagwan Shree Rajneesh On Basic Human Rights
The Book *An Introduction to theTeachings of Bhagwan Shree Rajneesh*
 Series I from A - H
 Series II from I - Q
 Series III from R - Z
Death: The Greatest Fiction
Gold Nuggets
The Greatest Challenge: The Golden Future
I Teach Religiousness Not Religion
Jesus Crucified Again, This Time in Ronald Reagan's America
Life, Love, Laughter
The New Man: The Only Hope for the Future
A New Vision of Women's Liberation
Priests and Politicians: The Mafia of the Soul
The Rebel: The Very Salt of the Earth
Sex: Quotations from Bhagwan Shree Rajneesh
Words from a Man of No Words

Photobiographies
Shree Rajneesh: A Man of Many Climates, Seasons and Rainbows
 Through the Eye of the Camera
The Sound of Running Water *Bhagwan Shree Rajneesh and His Work 1974-1978*
This Very Place The Lotus Paradise
 Bhagwan Shree Rajneesh and His Work 1978-1984

Books about Osho Rajneesh
Bhagwan Shree Rajneesh: The Most Dangerous Man
 Since Jesus Christ *(by Sue Appleton, LL.B.)*
Bhagwan: The Buddha For The Future *(by Juliet Forman, S.R.N., S.C.M., R.M.N.)*
Bhagwan: The Most Godless Yet The Most Godly Man
 (by Dr. George Meredith, M.D. M.B., B.S., M.R.C.P.)
Bhagwan: Twelve Days that Shook the World
 (by Juliet Forman, S.R.N., S.C.M., R.M.N.)
Was Bhagwan Shree Rajneesh Poisoned by Ronald Reagan's America?
 (by Sue Appleton, LL.B.)

ENGLISH LANGUAGE EDITIONS

OTHER PUBLISHERS

UNITED KINGDOM

The Art of Dying *(Sheldon Press)*
The Book of the Secrets *(Volume 1, Thames & Hudson)*
Dimensions Beyond the Known *(Sheldon Press)*
The Hidden Harmony *(Sheldon Press)*
Meditation: The Art of Ecstasy *(Sheldon Press)*
The Mustard Seed *(Sheldon Press)*
Neither This Nor That *(Sheldon Press)*
No Water, No Moon *(Sheldon Press)*
Roots and Wings *(Routledge & Kegan Paul)*
Straight to Freedom *(Original title: Until You Die, Sheldon Press)*
The Supreme Understanding
  (Original title: Tantra: The Supreme Understanding, Sheldon Press)
The Supreme Doctrine *(Routledge & Kegan Paul)*
Tao: The Three Treasures *(Volume 1, Wildwood House)*

Books about Osho Rajneesh

The Way of the Heart: the Rajneesh Movement
  by Judith Thompson and Paul Heelas, Department of Religious Studies,
  University of Lancaster (Aquarian Press)

UNITED STATES OF AMERICA

And the Flowers Showered *(De Vorss)*
The Book of the Secrets *(Volumes 1–3, Harper & Row)*
Dimensions Beyond the Known *(Wisdom Garden Books)*
The Grass Grows By Itself *(De Vorss)*
The Great Challenge *(Grove Press)*
Hammer on the Rock *(Grove Press)*
I Am the Gate *(Harper & Row)*
Journey Toward the Heart
  (Original title: Until You Die, Harper & Row)
Meditation: The Art of Ecstasy
  (Original title: Dynamics of Meditation, Harper & Row)
The Mustard Seed *(Harper & Row)*
My Way: The Way of the White Clouds *(Grove Press)*
Nirvana: The Last Nightmare *(Wisdom Garden Books)*
Only One Sky
  (Original title: Tantra: The Supreme Understanding, Dutton)
The Psychology of the Esoteric *(Harper & Row)*
Roots and Wings *(Routledge & Kegan Paul)*
The Supreme Doctrine *(Routledge & Kegan Paul)*
When the Shoe Fits *(De Vorss)*
Words Like Fire *(Original title: Come Follow Me, Volume 1, Harper & Row)*

Books about Osho Rajneesh

The Awakened One: The Life and Work of Bhagwan Shree Rajneesh
  by Vasant Joshi (Harper & Row)
Dying for Enlightenment by Bernard Gunther (Harper & Row)
Rajneeshpuram and the Abuse of Power by Ted Shay, Ph.D. (Scout Creek Press)
Rajneeshpuram, the Unwelcome Society by Kirk Braun (Scout Creek Press)
The Rajneesh Story: The Bhagwan's Garden
  by Dell Murphy (Linwood Press, Oregon)

FOREIGN LANGUAGE EDITIONS

Books by Osho Rajneesh have been translated and published
in the following languages:

Chinese	German	Japanese	Punjabi	Tamil
Czech	Greek	Korean	Russian	Telugu
Danish	Gujrati	Marathi	Serbo-Croat	Urdu
Dutch	Hebrew	Nepali	Sindhi	
Finnish	Hindi	Polish	Spanish	
French	Italian	Portuguese	Swedish	

Rajneesh Meditation Centers
Ashrams and Communes

There are many Rajneesh Meditation Centers throughout the world which can
be contacted for information about the teachings of Osho Rajneesh and
which have His books available as well as audio and video tapes of His
discourses. Centers exist in practically every country.

For further information about Osho Rajneesh

Rajneeshdham Neo-Sannyas Commune
17 Koregaon Park
Poona 411 001, MS
India